LONGMAN IMPRINT BOOKS

A Roald Dahl Selection

nine short stories by Roald Dahl

edited and introduced by
Roy Blatchford, BA
Bicester School, Oxon

with photographs by
Catherine Shakespeare Lane

KU-160-186

Longman

LONGMAN GROUP UK LIMITED
Longman House,
Burnt Mill, Harlow, Essex, CM20 2JE, England
and Associated Companies throughout the world.

"The Man from the South", "Lamb to the Slaughter", "Galloping
Foxley", "Skin" and "The Ratcatcher" are from *Someone Like
You*, originally published by Secker and Warburg Ltd in 1954 and
re-published by Michael Joseph Ltd in 1961. "The Landlady",
"The Champion of the World" and "Mrs Bixby and the Colonel's
Coat" are from *Kiss Kiss* first published by Michael Joseph Ltd in
1960.

© 1948, 1949, 1950, 1952, 1953, 1959, 1960 by Roald Dahl

This edition © Longman Group Limited 1980

All rights reserved; no part of this publication
may be reproduced, stored in a retrieval system, or
transmitted in any form or by any means, electronic,
mechanical, photocopying, recording or otherwise,
without the prior written permission of the Publishers.

This edition first published by Longman Group Limited
in association with Michael Joseph Limited 1960
Eighth impression 1987

ISBN 0 582 22281 8

Set in 10/11pt Baskerville 169

Produced by Longman Group (FE) Ltd
Printed in Hong Kong

We are grateful to Jonathan Cape Ltd for permission to
reproduce "The Hitchhiker" from *The Wonderful Story of Henry
Sugar*.

Contents

Introduction

"Fantastic" is perhaps the one word that best describes the
fictional world of Roald Dahl. To most readers he is probably
well known for the titles *Charlie and the Chocolate Factory* and
James and the Giant Peach. But in addition to his popular children's
novels – all of which have those unmistakable ingredients of
magic and uncanny fantasy – he has published nearly fifty
short stories for older readers. They range in length from five
to twenty-five pages and this volume's selection tries to present
not necessarily the nine very best, but a group of stories which
are varied in style and subject and guaranteed to entertain and
fascinate.

First and foremost the stories are here to be enjoyed. You
may want to leave them at that, content to be haunted by their
characters and plots long after you have closed the book, or you
may wish to spread the word that the stories of Roald Dahl
are a must to read. Yet it is also worthwhile studying these
intriguing tales to find out just what makes a good short story,
and how an outstanding writer practises the craft of fiction. At
the end of the book there are several pages of suggestions for
discussion and writing which you may wish to follow, together
with a section which examines Roald Dahl's stories and suggests
ways in which you can improve your own creative writing.

Roald Dahl was born in Wales of Norwegian parents, and
after a public school education (where at the age of fifteen his
report for English read: "A persistent muddler. Vocabulary
negligible, sentences mal-constructed. He reminds me of a
camel.") he served as a fighter pilot in the Second World War.
In 1942 he was posted to Washington D.C. as Assistant Air
Attaché and chanced to meet the great novelist C.S. Forester
who wanted ideas about flying stories. When Dahl wrote down
his thoughts in short story form Forester was so impressed with
their quality that he sent them straight to a magazine for
publication. Roald Dahl's writing career had begun.

In common with all writers his fiction springs from personal experience and the imagination; some of the tales in this selection mirror his first-hand knowledge of boarding schools, life in America and the adventures of a writer. But it is his extraordinary imagination which must account for the more bizarre, frightening, sinister and amusing exploits of his characters. You will quickly come to recognise Dahl's own style of describing scenes and people, the quiet rather ordinary openings to his stories, the gradual building up of tension, the simple twist of fate, the moments of horror and the ironic, artfully delayed endings.

Any reader will also come to recognize some of the author's favourite subjects and ideas. In "Man from the South" and "The Ratcatcher" there is his fascination with gambling; his preoccupation with the fantastic comes through in "The Champion of the World" and "The Hitchhiker"; his interest in the more distasteful side of flesh and blood is evident in "Skin" and "Lamb to the Slaughter"; there are the macabre deaths in "The Landlady"; while his great delight in ironically dashing expectations is there in "Mrs Bixby and the Colonel's Coat" and "Galloping Foxley".

It is Roald Dahl's great skill as a short story writer that he keeps his reader guessing. Could that really happen? Will the victim survive? What would I do in her place? In the tradition of thriller writers his plots will not allow us to put down the book until we reach that strange twist at the climax. The stories may frighten and sicken at one point, but at the next we smile at their humour and wry comment on human behaviour.

Above all, this selection is certain to whet a reader's appetite for more of the same.

R.B.

Man from the South

Man from the South

It was getting on towards six o'clock so I thought I'd buy myself a beer and go out and sit in a deckchair by the swimming pool and have a little evening sun.

I went to the bar and got the beer and carried it outside and wandered down the garden towards the pool.

It was a fine garden with lawns and beds of azaleas and tall coconut palms, and the wind was blowing strongly through the tops of the palm trees, making the leaves hiss and crackle as though they were on fire. I could see the clusters of big brown nuts hanging down underneath the leaves.

There were plenty of deck-chairs around the swimming pool and there were white tables and huge brightly coloured umbrellas and sunburned men and women sitting around in bathing suits. In the pool itself there were three or four girls and about a dozen boys, all splashing about and making a lot of noise and throwing a large rubber ball at one another.

I stood watching them. The girls were English girls from the hotel. The boys I didn't know about, but they sounded American, and I thought they were probably naval cadets who'd come ashore from the U.S. naval training vessel which had arrived in harbour that morning.

I went over and sat down under a yellow umbrella where there were four empty seats, and I poured my beer and settled back comfortably with a cigarette.

It was very pleasant sitting there in the sunshine with beer and cigarette. It was pleasant to sit and watch the bathers splashing about in the green water.

The American sailors were getting on nicely with the English girls. They'd reached the stage where they were diving under the water and tipping them up by their legs.

Just then I noticed a small, oldish man walking briskly around the edge of the pool. He was immaculately dressed in a white suit and he walked very quickly with little bouncing strides, pushing himself high up on to his toes with each step. He had on a large creamy Panama hat, and he came bouncing along the side of the pool, looking at the people and the chairs.

He stopped beside me and smiled, showing two rows of very small, uneven teeth, slightly tarnished.[1] I smiled back.

"Excuse pleess, but may I sit here?"

"Certainly," I said, "Go ahead."

He bobbed around to the back of the chair and inspected it for safety, then he sat down and crossed his legs. His white buckskin shoes had little holes punched all over them for ventilation.

"A fine evening," he said. "They are all evenings fine here in Jamaica." I couldn't tell if the accent were Italian or Spanish, but I felt fairly sure he was some sort of a South American. And old too, when you saw him close. Probably around sixty-eight or seventy.

"Yes," I said. "It is wonderful here, isn't it."

"And who, might I ask, are all dese? Dese is no hotel people." He was pointing at the bathers in the pool.

"I think they're American sailors," I told him. "They're Americans who are learning to be sailors."

"Of course dey are Americans. Who else in de world is going to make as much noise as dat? You are not American no?"

"No," I said. "I am not."

Suddenly one of the American cadets was standing in front of us. He was dripping wet from the pool and one of the English girls was standing there with him.

"Are these chairs taken?" he said.

"No," I answered.

"Mind if I sit down?"

"Go ahead."

"Thanks," he said. He had a towel in his hand and when he sat down he unrolled it and produced a pack of cigarettes and a lighter. He offered the cigarettes to the girl and she refused; then he offered them to me and I took one. The little man said, "Tank you, no but I tink I have a cigar." He pulled out a crocodile case and got himself a cigar, then he produced a knife which had a small scissors in it and he snipped the end off the cigar.

"Here, let me give you a light." The American boy held up his lighter.

"Dat will not work in dis wind."

---

[1] discoloured

"Sure it'll work. It always works."

The little man removed his unlighted cigar from his mouth, cocked his head on one side and looked at the boy.

"*All*-ways?" he said slowly.

"Sure, it never fails. Not with me anyway."

The little man's head was still cocked over on one side and he was still watching the boy. "Well, well. So you say dis famous lighter it never fails. Iss dat you say?"

"Sure," the boy said. "That's right." He was about nineteen or twenty with a long freckled face and a rather sharp birdlike nose. His chest was not very sunburned and there were freckles there too, and a few wisps of pale-reddish hair. He was holding the lighter in his right hand, ready to flip the wheel. "It never fails," he said, smiling now because he was purposely exaggerating his little boast. "I promise you it never fails."

"One momint, pleess." The hand that held the cigar came up high, palm outward, as though it were stopping traffic. "Now juss one momint." He had a curiously soft, toneless voice and he kept looking at the boy all the time.

"Shall we not perhaps make a little bet on dat?" He smiled at the boy. "Shall we not make a little bet on whether your lighter lights?"

"Sure, I'll bet," the boy said. "Why not?"

"You like to bet?"

"Sure, I'll always bet."

The man paused and examined his cigar, and I must say I didn't much like the way he was behaving. It seemed he was already trying to make something out of this, and to embarrass the boy, and at the same time I had the feeling he was relishing a private little secret all his own.

He looked up again at the boy and said slowly. "I like to bet, too. Why we don't have a good bet on dis ting? A good big bet."

"Now wait a minute," the boy said. "I can't do that. But I'll bet you a quarter. I'll even bet you a dollar, or whatever it is over here – some shillings, I guess."

The little man waved his hand again. "Listen to me. Now we have some fun. We make a bet. Den we go up to my room here in de hotel where iss no wind and I bet you you cannot light dis famous lighter of yours ten times running without missing once."

"I'll bet I can," the boy said.

"All right. Good. We make a bet, yes?"

"Sure, I'll bet you a buck."

"No, no. I make you a very good bet. I am rich man and I am sporting man also. Listen to me. Outside de hotel iss my car. Iss very fine car. American car from your country. Cadillac –"

"Hey, now. Wait a minute." The boy leaned back in his deck-chair and he laughed. "I can't put up that sort of property. This is crazy."

"Not crazy at all. You strike lighter successfully ten times running and Cadillac is yours. You like to have dis Cadillac, yes?"

"Sure, I'd like to have a Cadillac." The boy was still grinning.

"All right. Fine. We make a bet and I put up my Cadillac."

"And what do I put up?"

The little man carefully removed the red band from his still unlighted cigar. "I never ask you, my friend, to bet something you cannot afford. You understand?"

"Then what do I bet?"

"I make it very easy for you, yes?"

"Okay. You make it easy."

"Some small ting you can afford to give away, and if you did happen to lose it you would not feel too bad. Right?"

"Such as what?"

"Such as, perhaps, de little finger on your left hand."

"My *what*?" The boy stopped grinning.

"Yes. Why not? You win, you take de car. You looss, I take de finger."

"I don't get it. How d'you mean, you take the finger?"

"I chop it off."

"Jumping jeepers! That's a crazy bet. I think I'll just make it a dollar."

The little man leaned back, spread out his hands palms upwards and gave a tiny contemptuous shrug of the shoulders. "Well, well, well," he said. "I do not understand. You say it lights but you will not bet. Den we forget it, yes?"

The boy sat quite still, staring at the bathers in the pool. Then he remembered suddenly he hadn't lighted his cigarette. He put it between his lips, cupped his hands around the lighter and flipped the wheel. The wick lighted and burned with a small, steady, yellow flame and the way he held his hands the wind didn't get to it at all.

"Could I have a light, too?" I said.

"God, I'm sorry, I forgot you didn't have one."

5

I held out my hand for the lighter, but he stood up and came over to do it for me.

"Thank you," I said, and he returned to his seat.

"You having a good time?" I asked.

"Fine," he answered. "It's pretty nice here."

There was a silence then, and I could see that the little man had succeeded in disturbing the boy with his absurd proposal. He was sitting there very still, and it was obvious that a small tension was beginning to build up inside him. Then he started shifting about in his seat, and rubbing his chest, and stroking the back of his neck, and finally he placed both hands on his knees and began tap-tapping with his fingers against the knee-caps. Soon he was tapping with one of his feet as well.

"Now just let me check up on this bet of yours," he said at last. "You say we go up to your room and if I make this lighter light ten times running I win a Cadillac. If it misses just once then I forfeit the little finger of my left hand. Is that right?"

"Certainly. Dat is de bet. But I tink you are afraid."

"What do we do if I lose? Do I have to hold my finger out while you chop it off?"

"Oh, no! Dat would be no good. And you might be tempted to refuse to hold it out. What I should do I should tie one of your hands to de table before we started and I should stand dere with a knife ready to go *chop* de momint your lighter missed."

"What year is the Cadillac?" the boy asked.

"Excuse. I not understand."

"What year – how old is the Cadillac?"

"Ah! How old? Yes. It is last year. Quite new car. But I see you are not betting man. Americans never are."

The boy paused for just a moment and he glanced first at the English girl, then at me. "Yes," he said sharply. "I'll bet you."

"Good!" The little man clapped his hands together quietly, once. "Fine," he said. "We do it now. And you, sir," he turned to me, "you would perhaps be good enough to, what you call it, to – to referee." He had pale, almost colourless eyes with tiny bright black pupils.

"Well," I said. "I think it's a crazy bet. I don't think I like it very much."

"Nor do I," said the English girl. It was the first time she'd spoken. "I think it's a stupid, ridiculous bet."

"Are you serious about cutting off this boy's finger if he loses?" I said.

"Certainly I am. Also about giving him Cadillac if he win. Come now. We got to my room."

He stood up. "You like to put on some clothes first?" he said.

"No," the boy answered. "I'll come like this." Then he turned to me. "I'd consider it a favour if you'd come along and referee."

"All right," I said. "I'll come along, but I don't like the bet."

"You come too," he said to the girl. "You come and watch."

The little man led the way back through the garden to the hotel. He was animated now, and excited, and that seemed to make him bounce up higher than ever on his toes as he walked along.

"I live in annexe," he said. "You like to see car first? Iss just here."

He took us to where we could see the front driveway of the hotel and he stopped and pointed to a sleek pale-green Cadillac parked close by.

"Dere she iss. De green one. You like?"

"Say, that's a nice car," the boy said.

"All right. Now we go up and see if you can win her."

We followed him into the annexe and up one flight of stairs. He unlocked his door and we all trooped into what was a large pleasant double bedroom. There was a woman's dressing-gown lying across the bottom of one of the beds.

"First," he said, "we 'ave a little Martini."

The drinks were on a small table in the far corner, all ready to be mixed, and there was a shaker and ice and plenty of glasses. He began to make the Martini, but meanwhile he'd rung the bell and now there was a knock on the door and a coloured maid came in.

"Ah!" he said, putting down the bottle of gin, taking a wallet from his pocket and pulling out a pound note. "You will do something for me now, pleess." He gave the maid the pound.

"You keep dat," he said. "And now we are going to play a little game in here and I want you to go off and find for me two – no tree tings. I want some nails, I want a hammer, and I want a chopping knife, a butcher's chopping knife which you can borrow from de kitchen. You can get, yes?"

"A *chopping knife!*" The maid opened her eyes wide and clasped her hands in front of her. "You mean a *real* chopping knife?"

"Yes, yes, of course. Come on now, pleess. You can find dose tings surely for me."

7

"Yes, sir, I'll try, sir. Surely I'll try to get them." And she went.

The little man handed round the Martinis. We stood there and sipped them, the boy with the long freckled face and the pointed nose, bare-bodied except for a pair of faded brown bathing shorts: the English girl, a large-boned fair-haired girl wearing a pale blue bathing suit, who watched the boy over the top of her glass all the time; the little man with the colourless eyes standing there in his immaculate white suit drinking his Martini and looking at the girl in her pale blue bathing dress. I didn't know what to make of it all. The man seemed serious about the bet and he seemed serious about the business of cutting off the finger. But hell, what if the boy lost? Then we'd have to rush him to the hospital in the Cadillac that he hadn't won. That would be a fine thing. Now wouldn't that be a really fine thing? It would be a damn silly unnecessary thing so far as I could see.

"Don't you think this is rather a silly bet?" I said.

"I think it's a fine bet," the boy answered. He had already downed one large Martini.

"I think it's a stupid, ridiculous bet," the girl said. "What'll happen if you lost?"

"It won't matter. Come to think of it, I can't remember ever in my life having had any use for the little finger on my left hand. Here he is." The boy took hold of the finger. "Here he is and he hasn't ever done a thing for me yet. So why shouldn't I bet him? I think it's a fine bet."

The little man smiled and picked up the shaker and refilled our glasses.

"Before we begin," he said, "I will present to de – to de referee de key of de car." He produced a car key from his pocket and gave it to me. "De papers," he said, "de owning papers and insurance are in de pocket of de car."

Then the coloured maid came in again. In one hand she carried a small chopper, the kind used by butchers for chopping meat bones, and in the other a hammer and a bag of nails.

"Good! You get dem all. Tank you, tank you. Now you can go." He waited until the maid had closed the door, then he put the implements on one of the beds and said, "Now we prepare ourselves, yes?" And to the boy, "Help me, pleess, with dis table. We carry it out a little."

It was the usual kind of hotel writing desk, just a plain rectangular table about four feet by three with a blotting pad, ink, pens and paper. They carried it out into the room away from the wall, and removed the writing things.

"And now," he said, "a chair." He picked up a chair and placed it beside the table. He was very brisk and very animated, like a person organizing games at a children's party. "And now de nails. I must put in de nails." He fetched the nails and he began to hammer them into the top of the table.

We stood there, the boy, the girl, and I, holding Martinis in our hands, watching the little man at work. We watched him hammer two nails into the table, about six inches apart. He didn't hammer them right home; he allowed a small part of each one to stick up. Then he tested them for firmness with his fingers.

Anyone would think the son of a bitch had done this before, I told myself. He never hesitates. Table, nails, hammer, kitchen chopper. He knows exactly what he needs and how to arrange it.

"And now," he said, "all we want is some string." He found some string. "All right, at last we are ready. Will you pleess to sit here at de table?" he said to the boy.

The boy put his glass away and sat down.

"Now place de left hand between dese two nails. De nails are only so I can tie your hand in place. All right, good. Now I tie your hand secure to de table – so."

He wound the string around the boy's wrist, then several times around the wide part of the hand, then he fastened it tight to the nails. He made a good job of it and when he'd finished there wasn't any question about the boy being able to draw his hand away. But he could move his fingers.

"Now pleess, clench de fist, all except for de little finger. You must leave de little finger sticking out, lying on de table."

"*Ex*-cellent! *Ex*-cellent! Now we are ready. Wid your right hand you manipulate de lighter. But one momint, pleess."

He skipped over to the bed and picked up the chopper. He came back and stood beside the table with the chopper in his hand.

"We are all ready?" he said. "Mister referee, you must say to begin."

' The English girl was standing there in her pale blue bathing costume right behind the boy's chair. She was just standing there, not saying anything. The boy was sitting quite still, holding the lighter in his right hand, looking at the chopper. The little man was looking at me.

"Are you ready?" I asked the boy.

"I'm ready."

"And you?" to the little man.

"Quite ready," he said and he lifted the chopper up in the air and held it there about two feet above the boy's finger, ready to chop. The boy watched it, but he didn't flinch and his mouth didn't move at all. He merely raised his eyebrows and frowned.

"All right," I said. "Go ahead."

The boy said, "Will you please count aloud the number of times I light it."

"Yes," I said. "I'll do that."

With his thumb he raised the top of the lighter, and again with the thumb he gave the wheel a sharp flick. The flint sparked and the wick caught fire and burned with a small yellow flame.

"One!" I called.

He didn't blow the flame out; he closed the top of the lighter on it and he waited for perhaps five seconds before opening it again.

He flicked the wheel very strongly and once more there was a small flame burning on the wick.

"Two!"

No one else said anything. The boy kept his eyes on the lighter. The little man held the chopper up in the air and he too was watching the lighter.

"Three!"

"Four!"

"Five!"

"Six!"

"Seven!" Obviously it was one of those lighters that worked. The flint gave a big spark and the wick was the right length: I watched the thumb snapping the top down on to the flame. Then a pause. Then the thumb raising the top once more. This was an all-thumb operation. The thumb did everything. I took a breath, ready to say eight. The thumb flicked the wheel. The flint sparked. The little flame appeared.

"Eight!" I said, and as I said it the door opened. We all turned and we saw a woman standing in the doorway, a small, black-haired woman, rather old, who stood there for about two seconds then rushed forward, shouting, "Carlos! Carlos!" She grabbed his wrist, took the chopper from him, threw it on the bed, took hold of the little man by the lapels of his white suit and began shaking him very vigorously, talking to him fast and loud and fiercely all the time in some Spanish-sounding language. She shook him so fast you couldn't see him any more. He became a faint, misty, quickly moving outline, like the spokes of a turning wheel.

Then she slowed down and the little man came into view again and she hauled him across the room and pushed him backwards on to one of the beds. He sat on the edge of it blinking his eyes and testing his head to see if it would still turn on his neck.

"I am sorry," the woman said. "I am so terribly sorry that this should happen." She spoke almost perfect English.

"It is too bad," she went on. "I suppose it is really my fault. For ten minutes I leave him alone to go and have my hair washed and I come back and he is at it again." She looked sorry and deeply concerned.

The boy was untying his hand from the table. The English girl and I stood there and said nothing.

"He is a menace," the woman said. "Down where we live at home he has taken altogether forty-seven fingers from different people, and he has lost eleven cars. In the end they threatened to have him put away somewhere. That's why I brought him up here."

"We were only having a little bet," mumbled the little man from the bed.

"I suppose he bet you a car," the woman said.

"Yes," the boy answered. "A Cadillac."

"He has no car. It's mine. And that makes it worse," she said, "that he should bet you when he has nothing to bet with. I am ashamed and very sorry about it all." She seemed an awfully nice woman.

"Well," I said, "then here's the key of your car." I put it on the table.

"We were only having a little bet," mumbled the little man.

"He hasn't anything left to bet with," the woman said. "He hasn't a thing in the world. Not a thing. As a matter of fact I myself won it all from him a long while ago. It took time, a lot of time, and it was hard work, but I won it all in the end." She looked up at the boy and she smiled, a slow sad smile, and she came over and put out a hand to take the key from the table.

I can see it now, that hand of hers; it had only one finger on it, and a thumb.

Lamb to the Slaughter

Lamb to the Slaughter

The room was warm and clean, the curtains drawn, the two table lamps alight – hers and the one by the empty chair opposite. On the sideboard behind her, two tall glasses, soda water, whisky. Fresh ice cubes in the Thermos bucket.

Mary Maloney was waiting for her husband to come home from work.

Now and again she would glance up at the clock, but without anxiety, merely to please herself with the thought that each minute gone by made it nearer the time when he would come. There was a slow smiling air about her, and about everything she did. The drop of the head as she bent over her sewing was curiously tranquil. Her skin – for this was her sixth month with child – had acquired a wonderful translucent[1] quality, the mouth was soft, and the eyes, with their new placid look, seemed larger, darker than before.

When the clock said ten minutes to five, she began to listen, and a few moments later, punctually as always, she heard the tyres on the gravel outside, and the car door slamming, the footsteps passing the window, the key turning in the lock. She laid aside her sewing, stood up, and went forward to kiss him as he came in.

"Hullo, darling," she said.

"Hullo," he answered.

She took his coat and hung it in the closet. Then she walked over and made the drinks, a strongish one for him, a weak one for herself; and soon she was back again in her chair with the sewing, and he in the other, opposite, holding the tall glass with both his hands, rocking it so the ice cubes tinkled against the side.

For her, this was always a blissful time of day. She knew he didn't want to speak much until the first drink was finished, and she, on her side, was content to sit quietly, enjoying his

[1] shining

company after the long hours alone in the house. She loved to luxuriate in the presence of this man, and to feel – almost as a sunbather feels the sun – that warm male glow that came out of him to her when they were alone together. She loved him for the way he sat loosely in a chair, for the way he came in a door, or moved slowly across the room with long strides. She loved the intent, far look in his eyes when they rested on her, the funny shape of the mouth, and especially the way he remained silent about his tiredness, sitting still with himself until the whisky had taken some of it away.

"Tired, darling?"

"Yes," he said. "I'm tired." And as he spoke, he did an unusual thing. He lifted his glass and drained it in one swallow although there was still half of it, at least half of it, left. She wasn't really watching him but she knew what he had done because she heard the ice cubes falling back against the bottom of the empty glass when he lowered his arm. He paused a moment, leaning forward in the chair, then he got up and went slowly over to fetch himself another.

"I'll get it!" she cried, jumping up.

"Sit down," he said.

When he came back, she noticed that the new drink was dark amber with the quantity of whisky in it.

"Darling, shall I get your slippers?"

"No."

She watched him as he began to sip the dark yellow drink, and she could see little oily swirls in the liquid because it was so strong.

"I think it's a shame," she said, "that when a policeman gets to be as senior as you, they keep him walking about on his feet all day long."

He didn't answer, so she bent her head again and went on with her sewing; but each time he lifted the drink to his lips, she heard the ice cubes clinking against the side of the glass.

"Darling," she said. "Would you like me to get you some cheese? I haven't made any supper because it's Thursday."

"No," he said.

"If you're too tired to eat out," she went on, "it's still not too late. There's plenty of meat and stuff in the freezer, and you can have it right here and not even move out of the chair."

Her eyes waited on him for an answer, a smile, a little nod, but he made no sign.

"Anyway," she went on, "I'll get you some cheese and crackers first."

"I don't want it," he said.

She moved uneasily in her chair, the large eyes still watching his face. "But you *must* have supper. I can easily do it here. I'd like to do it. We can have lamb chops. Or pork. Anything you want. Everything's in the freezer."

"Forget it," he said.

"But, darling, you *must* eat! I'll fix it anyway, and then you can have it or not, as you like."

She stood up and placed her sewing on the table by the lamp.

"Sit down," he said. "Just for a minute, sit down."

It wasn't till then that she began to get frightened.

"Go on," he said. "Sit down."

She lowered herself back slowly into the chair, watching him all the time with those large, bewildered eyes. He had finished the second drink and was staring down into the glass, frowning.

"Listen," he said, "I've got something to tell you."

"What is it, darling? What's the matter?"

He had become absolutely motionless, and he kept his head down so that the light from the lamp beside him fell across the upper part of his face, leaving the chin and mouth in shadow. She noticed there was a little muscle moving near the corner of his left eye.

"This is going to be a bit of a shock to you, I'm afraid," he said. "But I've thought about it a good deal and I've decided the only thing to do is tell you right away. I hope you won't blame me too much."

And he told her. It didn't take long, four or five minutes at most, and she sat very still through it all, watching him with a kind of dazed horror as he went further and further away from her with each word.

"So there it is," he added. "And I know it's kind of a bad time to be telling you, but there simply wasn't any other way. Of course I'll give you money and see you're looked after. But there needn't really be any fuss. I hope not anyway. It wouldn't be very good for my job."

Her first instinct was not to believe any of it, to reject it all. It occurred to her that perhaps he hadn't even spoken, that she herself had imagined the whole thing. Maybe, if she went about her business and acted as though she hadn't been listening,

16

then later, when she sort of woke up again, she might find none of it had ever happened.

"I'll get the supper," she managed to whisper, and this time he didn't stop her.

When she walked across the room she couldn't feel her feet touching the floor. She couldn't feel anything at all – except a slight nausea and a desire to vomit. Everything was automatic now – down the stairs to the cellar, the light switch, the deep freeze, the hand inside the cabinet taking hold of the first object it met. She lifted it out, and looked at it. It was wrapped in paper, so she took off the paper and looked at it again.

A leg of lamb.

All right then, they would have lamb for supper. She carried it upstairs, holding the thin bone-end of it with both her hands, and as she went through the living-room, she saw him standing over by the window with his back to her, and she stopped.

"For God's sake," he said, hearing her, but not turning round, "Don't make supper for me. I'm going out."

At that point, Mary Maloney simply walked up behind him and without any pause she swung the big frozen leg of lamb high in the air and brought it down as hard as she could on the back of his head.

She might just as well have hit him with a steel club.

She stepped back a pace, waiting, and the funny thing was that he remained standing there for at least four or five seconds, gently swaying. Then he crashed to the carpet.

The violence of the crash, the noise, the small table over-turning, helped bring her out of the shock. She came out slowly, feeling cold and surprised, and she stood for a while blinking at the body, still holding the ridiculous piece of meat tight with both hands.

All right, she told herself. So I've killed him.

It was extraordinary, now, how clear her mind became all of a sudden. She began thinking very fast. As the wife of a detective, she knew quite well what the penalty would be. That was fine. It made no difference to her. In fact, it would be a relief. On the other hand, what about the child? What were the laws about murderers with unborn children? Did they kill them both – mother and child? Or did they wait until the tenth month? What did they do?

Mary Maloney didn't know. And she certainly wasn't pre-pared to take a chance.

She carried the meat into the kitchen, placed it in a pan, turned the oven on high, and shoved it inside. Then she washed her hands and ran upstairs to the bedroom. She sat down before the mirror, tidied her face, touched up her lips and face. She tried a smile. It came out rather peculiar. She tried again.

"Hullo Sam," she said brightly, aloud.

The voice sounded peculiar too.

"I want some potatoes please, Sam. Yes, and I think a can of peas."

That was better. Both the smile and the voice were coming out better now. She rehearsed it several times more. Then she ran downstairs, took her coat, went out the back door, down the garden, into the street.

It wasn't six o'clock yet and the lights were still on in the grocery shop.

"Hullo Sam," she said brightly, smiling at the man behind the counter.

"Why, good evening, Mrs Maloney. How're *you?*"

"I want some potatoes please, Sam. Yes, and I think a can of peas."

The man turned and reached up behind him on the shelf for the peas.

"Patrick's decided he's tired and doesn't want to eat out tonight," she told him. "We usually go out Thursdays, you know, and now he's caught me without any vegetables in the house."

"Then how about meat, Mrs Maloney?"

"No, I've got meat, thanks. I got a nice leg of lamb, from the freezer."

"Oh."

"I don't much like cooking it frozen, Sam, but I'm taking a chance on it this time. You think it'll be all right?"

"Personally," the grocer said, "I don't believe it makes any difference. You want these Idaho potatoes?"

"Oh yes, that'll be fine. Two of those."

"Anything else?" The grocer cocked his head on one side, looking at her pleasantly. "How about afterwards? What you going to give him for afterwards?"

"Well – what would you suggest, Sam?"

The man glanced around his shop. "How about a nice big slice of cheesecake? I know he likes that."

"Perfect," she said. "He loves it."

And when it was all wrapped and she had paid, she put on her brightest smile and said, "Thank you, Sam. Good night."

"Good night, Mrs Maloney. And thank *you*."

And now, she told herself as she hurried back, all she was doing now, she was returning home to her husband and he was waiting for his supper; and she must cook it good, and make it as tasty as possible because the poor man was tired; and if, when she entered the house, she happened to find anything unusual, or tragic, or terrible, then naturally it would be a shock and she'd become frantic with grief and horror. Mind you, she wasn't *expecting* to find anything. She was just going home with the vegetables. Mrs Patrick Maloney going home with the vegetables on Thursday evening to cook supper for her husband.

That's the way, she told herself. Do everything right and natural. Keep things absolutely natural and there'll be no need for any acting at all.

Therefore, when she entered the kitchen by the back door, she was humming a little tune to herself and smiling.

"Patrick!" she called. "How are you, darling?"

She put the parcel down on the table and went through into the living-room; and when she saw him lying there on the floor with his legs doubled up and one arm twisted back underneath his body, it really was rather a shock. All the old love and longing for him welled up inside her, and she ran over to him, knelt down beside him, and began to cry her heart out. It was easy. No acting was necessary.

A few minutes later she got up and went to the phone. She knew the number of the police station, and when the man at the other end answered, she cried to him, "Quick! Come quick! Patrick's dead!"

"Who's speaking?"

"Mrs Maloney. Mrs Patrick Maloney."

"You mean Patrick Maloney's dead?"

"I think so," she sobbed. "He's lying on the floor and I think he's dead."

"Be right over," the man said.

The car came very quickly, and when she opened the front door, two policemen walked in. She knew them both – she knew nearly all the men at that precinct – and she fell right into Jack Noonan's arms, weeping hysterically. He put her gently into a chair, then went over to join the other one, who was called O'Malley, kneeling by the body.

"Is he dead?" she cried.

"I'm afraid he is. What happened?"

Briefly, she told her story about going out to the grocer and coming back to find him on the floor. While she was talking, crying and talking, Noonan discovered a small patch of congealed blood on the dead man's head. He showed it to O'Malley who got up at once and hurried to the phone.

Soon, other men began to come into the house. First a doctor, then two detectives, one of whom she knew by name. Later, a police photographer arrived and took pictures, and a man who knew about fingerprints. There was a great deal of whispering and muttering beside the corpse, and the detectives kept asking her a lot of questions. But they always treated her kindly. She told her story again, this time right from the beginning, when Patrick had come in, and she was sewing, and he was tired, so tired he hadn't wanted to go out for supper. She told how she'd put the meat in the oven – "it's there now, cooking" – and how she'd slipped out to the grocer for vegetables, and come back to find him lying on the floor.

"Which grocer?" one of the detectives asked.

She told him, and he turned and whispered something to the other detective who immediately went outside into the street.

In fifteen minutes he was back with a page of notes, and there was more whispering, and through her sobbing she heard a few of the whispered phrases – "... acted quite normal ... very cheerful ... wanted to give him a good supper ... peas ... cheesecake ... impossible that she ..."

After a while, the photographer and the doctor departed and two other men came in and took the corpse away on a stretcher. Then the fingerprint man went away. The two detectives remained, and so did the two policemen. They were exceptionally nice to her, and Jack Noonan asked if she wouldn't rather go somewhere else, to her sister's house perhaps, or to his own wife who would take care of her and put her up for the night.

No, she said, She didn't feel she could move even a yard at the moment. Would they mind awfully if she stayed just where she was until she felt better? She didn't feel too good at the moment, she really didn't.

Then hadn't she better lie down on the bed? Jack Noonan asked.

No, she said, she'd like to stay right where she was, in this chair. A little later perhaps, when she felt better, she would move.

So they left her there while they went about their business, searching the house. Occasionally one of the detectives asked her another question. Sometimes Jack Noonan spoke to her gently as he passed by. Her husband, he told her, had been killed by a blow on the back of the head administered with a heavy blunt instrument, almost certainly a large piece of metal. They were looking for the weapon. The murderer may have taken it with him, but on the other hand he may've thrown it away or hidden it somewhere on the premises.

"It's the old story," he said. "Get the weapon, and you've got the man."

Later, one of the detectives came up and sat beside her. Did she know, he asked, of anything in the house that could've been used as the weapon? Would she mind having a look around to see if anything was missing – a very big spanner, for example, or a heavy metal vase.

They didn't have any heavy metal vases, she said.

"Or a big spanner?"

She didn't think they had a big spanner. But there might be some things like that in the garage.

The search went on. She knew that there were other police-men in the garden all around the house. She could hear their footsteps on the gravel outside, and sometimes she saw the flash of a torch through a chink in the curtains. It began to get late, nearly nine she noticed by the clock on the mantel. The four men searching the rooms seemed to be growing weary, a trifle exasperated.[1]

"Jack," she said, the next time Sergeant Noonan went by. "Would you mind giving me a drink?"

"Sure I'll give you a drink. You mean this whisky?"

"Yes, please. But just a small one. It might make me feel better."

He handed her the glass.

"Why don't you have one yourself," she said. "You must be awfully tired. Please do. You've been very good to me."

"Well," he answered. "It's not strictly allowed, but I might take just a drop to keep me going."

One by one the others came in and were persuaded to take a

[1] irritated

little nip of whisky. They stood around rather awkwardly with the drinks in their hands, uncomfortable in her presence, trying to say consoling things to her. Sergeant Noonan wandered into the kitchen, came out quickly and said, "Look, Mrs Maloney." You know that oven of yours is still on, and the meat still inside."

"Oh *dear* me!" she cried. "So it is!"

"I better turn it off for you, hadn't I?"

"Will you do that, Jack. Thank you so much."

When the sergeant returned the second time, she looked at him with her large, dark, tearful eyes. "Jack Noonan," she said.

"Yes?"

"Would you do me a small favour – you and these others?"

"We can try, Mrs Maloney."

"Well," she said. "Here you all are, and good friends of dear Patrick's too, and helping to catch the man who killed him. You must be terrible hungry by now because it's long past your supper time, and I know Patrick would never forgive me, God bless his soul, if I allowed you to remain in his house without offering you decent hospitality. Why don't you eat up that lamb that's in the oven? It'll be cooked just right by now."

"Wouldn't dream of it," Sergeant Noonan said.

"Please," she begged. "Please eat it. Personally I couldn't touch a thing, certainly not what's been in the house when he was here. But it's all right for you. It'd be a favour to me if you'd eat it up. Then you can go on with your work again afterwards."

There was a good deal of hesitating among the four policemen, but they were clearly hungry, and in the end they were per-suaded to go into the kitchen and help themselves. The woman stayed where she was, listening to them through the open door, and she could hear them speaking among themselves, their voices thick and sloppy because their mouths were full of meat.

"Have some more, Charlie?"

"No. Better not finish it."

"She *wants* us to finish it. She said so. Be doing her a favour."

"Okay then. Give me some more."

"That's the hell of a big club the guy must've used to hit poor Patrick," one of them was saying. "The doc says his skull was smashed all to pieces just like from a sledge-hammer."

"That's why it ought to be easy to find."

"Exactly what I say."

"Whoever done it, they're not going to be carrying a thing like that around with them longer than they need."

One of them belched.

"Personally, I think it's right here on the premises."

"Probably right under our very noses. What you think Jack?"

And in the other room, Mary Maloney began to giggle.

The Landlady

The Landlady

Billy Weaver had travelled down from London on the slow afternoon train, with a change at Swindon on the way, and by the time he got to Bath it was about nine o'clock in the evening and the moon was coming up out of a clear starry sky over the houses opposite the station entrance. But the air was deadly cold and the wind was like a flat blade of ice on his cheeks.

"Excuse me," he said, "but is there a fairly cheap hotel not too far away from here?"

"Try The Bell and Dragon," the porter answered, pointing down the road. "They might take you in. It's about a quarter of a mile along on the other side."

Billy thanked him and picked up his suitcase and set out to walk the quarter-mile to The Bell and Dragon. He had never been to Bath before. He didn't know anyone who lived there. But Mr Greenslade at the Head Office in London had told him it was a splendid city. "Find your own lodgings," he had said, "and then go along and report to the Branch Manager as soon as you've got yourself settled."

Billy was seventeen years old. He was wearing a new navy-blue overcoat, a new brown trilby hat, and a new brown suit, and he was feeling fine. He walked briskly down the street. He was trying to do everything briskly these days. Briskness, he had decided, was *the* one common characteristic of all successful businessmen. The big shots up at Head Office were absolutely fantastically brisk all the time. They were amazing.

There were no shops on this wide street that he was walking along, only a line of tall houses on each side, all of them identical. They had porches and pillars and four or five steps going up to their front doors, and it was obvious that once upon a time they had been very swanky residences. But now, even in the darkness, he could see that the paint was peeling from the woodwork on their doors and windows, and that the handsome white façades[1]

---

[1] house-fronts

were cracked and blotchy from neglect.

Suddenly, in a downstairs window that was brilliantly illuminated by a street-lamp not six yards away, Billy caught sight of a printed notice propped up against the glass in one of the upper panes. It said BED AND BREAKFAST. There was a vase of pussywillows, tall and beautiful, standing just underneath the notice.

He stopped walking. He moved a bit closer. Green curtains (some sort of velvety material) were hanging down on either side of the window. The pussy-willows looked wonderful beside them. He went right up and peered through the glass into the room, and the first thing he saw was a bright fire burning in the hearth. On the carpet in front of the fire, a pretty little dachshund was curled up asleep with its nose tucked into its belly. The room itself, so far as he could see in the half-darkness, was filled with pleasant furniture. There was a baby-grand piano and a big sofa and several plump armchairs; and in one corner he spotted a large parrot in a cage. Animals were usually a good sign in a place like this, Billy told himself; and all in all, it looked to him as though it would be a pretty decent house to stay in. Certainly it would be more comfortable than The Bell and Dragon.

On the other hand, a pub would be more congenial than a boarding-house. There would be beer and darts in the evenings, and lots of people to talk to, and it would probably be a good bit cheaper, too. He had stayed a couple of nights in a pub once before and he had liked it. He had never stayed in any boarding-houses, and, to be perfectly honest, he was a tiny bit frightened of them. The name itself conjured up images of watery cabbage, rapacious[1] landladies, and a powerful smell of kippers in the living-room.

After dithering about like this in the cold for two or three minutes, Billy decided that he would walk on and take a look at The Bell and Dragon before making up his mind. He turned to go.

And now a queer thing happened to him. He was in the act of stepping back and turning away from the window when all at once his eye was caught and held in the most peculiar manner by the small notice that was there. BED AND BREAKFAST, it said. BED AND BREAKFAST, BED AND BREAKFAST, BED AND BREAKFAST.

[1] greedy

27

Each word was like a large black eye staring at him through the glass, holding him, compelling him, forcing him to stay where he was and not to walk away from that house, and the next thing he knew, he was actually moving across from the window to the front door of the house, climbing the steps that led up to it, and reaching for the bell.

He pressed the bell. Far away in a back room he heard it ringing, and then *at once* – it must have been at once because he hadn't even had time to take his finger from the bell-button – the door swung open and a woman was standing there.

Normally you ring the bell and you have at least a half-minute's wait before the door opens. But this dame was like a jack-in-the-box. He pressed the bell – and out she popped! It made him jump.

She was about forty-five or fifty years old, and the moment she saw him, she gave him a warm welcoming smile.

"*Please* come in," she said pleasantly. She stepped aside, holding the door wide open, and Billy found himself automatically starting forward into the house. The compulsion or, more accurately, the desire to follow after her into that house was extraordinarily strong.

"I saw the notice in the window," he said, holding himself back.

"Yes, I know."

"I was wondering about a room."

"It's *all* ready for you, my dear," she said. She had a round pink face and very gentle blue eyes.

"I was on my way to The Bell and Dragon," Billy told her. "But the notice in your window just happened to catch my eye."

"My dear boy," she said, "why don't you come in out of the cold?"

"How much do you charge?"

"Five and sixpence a night, including breakfast."

It was fantastically cheap. It was less than half of what he had been willing to pay.

"If that is too much," she added, "then perhaps I can reduce it just a tiny bit. Do you desire an egg for breakfast? Eggs are expensive at the moment. It would be sixpence less without the egg."

"Five and sixpence is fine," he answered. "I should like very much to stay here."

"I knew you would. Do come in."

She seemed terribly nice. She looked exactly like the mother of one's best school-friend welcoming one into the house to stay for the Christmas holidays. Billy took off his hat, and stepped over the threshold.

"Just hang it there," she said, "and let me help you with your coat."

There were no other hats or coats in the hall. There were no umbrellas, no walking-sticks – nothing.

"We have it *all* to ourselves," she said, smiling at him over her shoulder as she led the way upstairs. "You see, it isn't very often I have the pleasure of taking a visitor into my little nest."

The old girl is slightly dotty, Billy told himself. But at five and sixpence a night, who gives a damn about that? 'I should've thought you'd be simply swamped with applicants," he said politely.

"Oh, I am, my dear, I am, of course I am. But the trouble is that I'm inclined to be just a teeny weeny bit choosy and parti-cular – if you see what I mean."

"Ah, yes."

"But I'm always ready. Everything is always ready day and night in this house just on the off-chance that an acceptable young gentleman will come along. And it is such a pleasure, my dear, such a very great pleasure when now and again I open the door and I see someone standing there who is just *exactly* right." She was half-way up the stairs, and she paused with one hand on the stair-rail, turning her head and smiling down at him with pale lips. "Like you," she added, and her blue eyes travelled slowly all the way down the length of Billy's body, to his feet, and then up again.

On the first-floor landing she said to him, "This floor is mine."

They climbed up a second flight. "And this one is *all* yours," she said. "Here's your room. I do hope you'll like it." She took him into a small but charming front bedroom, switching on the light as she went in.

'The morning sun comes right in the window, Mr Perkins. It *is* Mr Perkins, isn't it?"

"No," he said. "It's Weaver."

"Mr Weaver. How nice. I've put a water-bottle between the sheets to air them out, Mr Weaver. It's such a comfort to have a hot water-bottle in a strange bed with clean sheets, don't you agree? And you may light the gas fire at any time if you feel chilly."

"Thank you," Billy said. "Thank you ever so much." He noticed that the bedspread had been taken off the bed, and that the bedclothes had been neatly turned back on one side, all ready for someone to get in.

'I'm so glad you appeared," she said, looking earnestly into his face. "I was beginning to get worried."

"That's all right," Billy answered brightly. "You mustn't worry about me." He put his suitcase on the chair and started to open it.

"And what about supper, my dear? Did you manage to get anything to eat before you came here?"

"I'm not a bit hungry, thank you," he said. "I think I'll just go to bed as soon as possible because tomorrow I've got to get up rather early and report to the office."

"Very well, then. I'll leave you now so that you can unpack. But before you go to bed, would you be kind enough to pop into the sitting-room on the ground floor and sign the book? Everyone has to do that because it's the law of the land, and we don't want to go breaking any laws at *this* stage in the proceedings, do we?" She gave him a little wave of the hand and went quickly out of the room and closed the door.

Now, the fact that his landlady appeared to be slightly off her rocker didn't worry Billy in the least. After all, she was not only harmless – there was no question about that – but she was also quite obviously a kind and generous soul. He guessed that she had probably lost a son in the war, or something like that, and had never got over it.

So a few minutes later, after unpacking his suitcase and washing his hands, he trotted downstairs to the ground floor and entered the living-room. His landlady wasn't there, but the fire was glowing in the hearth, and the little dachshund was still sleeping in front of it. The room was wonderfully warm and cosy. I'm a lucky fellow, he thought, rubbing his hands. This is a bit of all right.

He found the guest-book lying open on the piano, so he took out his pen and wrote down his name and address. There were only two other entries above his on the page, and, as one always does with guest-books, he started to read them. One was a Christopher Mulholland from Cardiff. The other was Gregory W. Temple from Bristol.

That's funny, he thought suddenly. Christopher Mulholland. It rings a bell.

Now where on earth had he heard that rather unusual name before?

Was he a boy at school? No. Was it one of his sister's numerous young men, perhaps, or a friend of his father's? No, no, it wasn't any of those. He glanced down again at the book.

> Christopher Mulholland   231 Cathedral Road, Cardiff
> Gregory W. Temple   27 Sycamore Drive, Bristol

As a matter of fact, now he came to think of it, he wasn't at all sure that the second name didn't have almost as much of a familiar ring about it as the first.

"Gregory Temple?" he said aloud, searching his memory. "Christopher Mulholland? . . . "

"Such charming boys," a voice behind him answered, and he turned and saw his landlady sailing into the room with a large silver tea-tray in her hands. She was holding it well out in front of her, and rather high up, as though the tray were a pair of reins on a frisky horse.

"They sound somehow familiar," he said.

"They do? How interesting."

"I'm almost positive I've heard those names before somewhere. Isn't that queer? Maybe it was in the newspapers. They weren't famous in any way, were they? I mean famous cricketers or footballers or something like that?"

"Famous," she said, setting the tea-tray down on the low table in front of the sofa. "Oh no, I don't think they were famous. But they were extraordinarily handsome, both of them, I can promise you that. They were tall and young and handsome, my dear, just exactly like you."

Once more, Billy glanced down at the book. "Look here," he said, noticing the dates. "This last entry is over two years old."

"It is?"

"Yes, indeed. And Christopher Mulholland's is nearly a year before that – more than *three years* ago."

"Dear me," she said, shaking her head and heaving a dainty little sigh. "I would never have thought it. How time does fly away from us all, doesn't it, Mr Wilkins?"

"It's Weaver," Billy said. "W-e-a-v-e-r."

"Oh, of course it is?" she cried, sitting down on the sofa. "How silly of me. I do apologize. In one ear and out the other, that's me, Mr Weaver."

"You know something?" Billy said. "Something that's really quite extraordinary about all this?"

"No, dear, I don't."

"Well, you see – both of these names, Mulholland and Temple, I not only seem to remember each one of them separately, so to speak, but somehow or other, in some peculiar way, they both appear to be sort of connected together as well. As though they were both famous for the same sort of thing, if you see what I mean – like ... well ... like Dempsey and Tunney,[1] for example, or Churchill and Roosevelt."[2]

"How amusing," she said. "But come over here now, dear, and sit down beside me on the sofa and I'll give you a nice cup of tea and a ginger biscuit before you to to bed."

"You really shouldn't bother," Billy said. "I didn't mean you to do anything like that." He stood by the piano, watching her as she fussed about with the cups and saucers. He noticed that she had small, white, quickly moving hands, and red finger-nails.

"I'm almost positive it was in the newspapers I saw them," Billy said. "I'll think of it in a second. I'm sure I will."

There is nothing more tantalizing than a thing like this which lingers just outside the borders of one's memory. He hated to give up.

"Now wait a minute," he said. "Wait just a minute. Mulholland ... Christopher Mulholland ... wasn't *that* the name of the Eton schoolboy who was on a walking-tour through the West Country, and then all of a sudden ... "

"Milk?" she said. "And sugar?"

"Yes, please. And then all of a sudden ... "

"Eton schoolboy?" she said, "Oh no, my dear, that can't possibly be right because *my* Mr Mulholland was certainly not an Eton schoolboy when he came to me. He was a Cambridge undergraduate. Come over here now and sit next to me and warm yourself in front of this lovely fire. Come on. Your tea's all ready for you." She patted the empty place beside her on the sofa, and she sat there smiling at Billy and waiting for him to come over.

He crossed the room slowly, and sat down on the edge of the sofa. She placed his teacup on the table in front of him.

[1] famous boxers
[2] political leaders

"*There* we are," she said. "How nice and cosy this is, isn't it?"

Billy started sipping his tea. She did the same. For half a minute or so, neither of them spoke. But Billy knew that she was looking at him. Her body was half-turned towards him and he could feel her eyes resting on his face, watching him over the rim of her teacup. Now and again, he caught a whiff of a peculiar smell that seemed to emanate[1] directly from her person. It was not in the least unpleasant, and it reminded him – well, he wasn't quite sure what it reminded him of. Pickled walnuts? New leather? Or was it the corridors of a hospital?

"Mr Mullholland was a great one for his tea," she said at length. "Never in my life have I seen anyone drink as much tea as dear, sweet Mr Mulholland."

"I suppose he left fairly recently," Billy said. He was still puzzling his head about the two names. He was positive now that he had seen them in the newspapers – in the headlines.

"Left?" she said, arching her brows. "But my dear boy, he never left. He's still here. Mr Temple is also here. They're on the third floor, both of them together."

Billy set down his cup slowly on the table, and stared at his landlady. She smiled back at him, and then she put out one of her white hands and patted him comfortingly on the knee. "How old are you, my dear?" she asked.

"Seventeen."

"Seventeen!" she cried. "Oh, it's the perfect age! Mr Mulholland was also seventeen. But I think he was a trifle shorter than you are, in fact I'm sure he was, and his teeth weren't *quite* so white. You have the most beautiful teeth, Mr Weaver, did you know that?"

"They're not as good as they look," Billy said. "They've got simply masses of fillings in them at the back."

"Mr Temple, of course, was a little older," she said, ignoring his remark. "He was actually twenty-eight. And yet I never would have guessed it if he hadn't told me, never in my whole life. There wasn't a *blemish* on his body."

"A what?" Billy said.

"His skin was *just* like a baby's."

There was a pause. Billy picked up his teacup and took another sip of his tea, then he set it down again gently in its saucer. He waited for her to say something else, but she seemed

[1] flow

to have lapsed into another of her silences. He sat there staring ahead of him into the far corner of the room, biting his lower lip.

"That parrot," he said at last. "You know something? It had me completely fooled when I first saw it through the window from the street. I could have sworn it was alive."

"Alas, no longer."

"It's most terribly clever the way it's been done," he said. "It doesn't look in the least bit dead. Who did it?"

"I did."

"*You* did?"

"Of course," she said. "And have you met my little Basil as well?" She nodded towards the dachshund curled up so comfortably in front of the fire. Billy looked at it. And suddenly, he realized that this animal had all the time been just as silent and motionless as the parrot. He put out a hand and touched it gently on the top of its back. The back was hard and cold, and when he pushed the hair to one side with his fingers, he could see the skin underneath, greyish-black and dry and perfectly preserved.

"Good gracious me," he said. "How absolutely fascinating." He turned away from the dog and stared with deep admiration at the little woman beside him on the sofa. "It must be most awfully difficult to do a thing like that."

"Not in the least," she said. "I stuff *all* my little pets myself when they pass away. Will you have another cup of tea?"

"No, thank you," Billy said. The tea tasted faintly of bitter almonds, and he didn't much care for it.

"You did sign the book, didn't you?"

"Oh, yes."

"That's good. Because later on, if I happen to forget what you were called, then I can always come down here and look it up. I still do that almost every day with Mr Mulholland and Mr . . . Mr . . . "

"Temple," Billy said. "Gregory Temple. Excuse my asking, but haven't there been *any* other guests here except them in the last two or three years?"

Holding her teacup high in one hand, inclining her head slightly to the left, she looked up at him out of the corners of her eyes and gave him another gentle little smile.

"No, my dear," she said. "Only you."

The
Champion
of the
World

The Champion of the World

All day, in between serving customers, we had been crouching over the table in the office of the filling-station, preparing the raisins. They were plump and soft and swollen from being soaked in water, and when you nicked them with a razor-blade the skin sprang open and the jelly stuff inside squeezed out as easily as you could wish.

But we had a hundred and ninety-six of them to do altogether and the evening was nearly upon us before we had finished.

'Don't they look marvellous!' Claud cried, rubbing his hands together hard. "What time is it, Gordon?"

"Just after five."

Through the window we could see a station-wagon pulling up at the pumps with a woman at the wheel and about eight children in the back eating ice-creams.

"We ought to be moving soon," Claud said. "The whole thing'll be a washout if we don't arrive before sunset, you realize that." He was getting twitchy now. His face had the same flushed and pop-eyed look it got before a dog-race or when there was a date with Clarice in the evening.

We both went outside and Claud gave the woman the number of gallons she wanted. When she had gone, he remained standing in the middle of the driveway squinting anxiously up at the sun which was now only the width of a man's hand above the line of trees along the crest of the ridge on the far side of the valley.

"All right," I said. "Lock up."

He went quickly from pump to pump, securing each nozzle in its holder with a small padlock.

"You'd better take off that yellow pullover," he said.

"Why should I?"

"You'll be shining like a bloody beacon out there in the moonlight."

"I'll be all right."

"You will not," he said. "Take it off, Gordon, please. I'll see you in three minutes." He disappeared into his caravan behind the filling-station, and I went indoors and changed my yellow pullover for a blue one.

When we met again outside, Claud was dressed in a pair of black trousers and a dark-green turtleneck sweater. On his head he wore a brown cloth cap with the peak pulled down low over his eyes, and he looked like an apache actor out of a nightclub.

"What's under there?" I asked, seeing the bulge at his waistline.

He pulled up his sweater and showed me two thin but very large white cotton sacks which were bound neat and tight around his belly. "To carry the stuff," he said darkly.

"I see."

"Let's go," he said.

"I still think we ought to take the car."

"It's too risky. They'll see it parked."

"But it's over three miles up to that wood."

"Yes," he said. "And I suppose you realize we can get six months in the clink if they catch us."

"You never told me that."

"Didn't I?"

"I'm not coming," I said. "It's not worth it."

"The walk will do you good, Gordon. Come on."

It was a calm sunny evening with little wisps of brilliant white cloud hanging motionless in the sky, and the valley was cool and very quiet as the two of us began walking together along the grass verge on the side of the road that ran between the hills towards Oxford.

"You got the raisins?" Claud asked.

"They're in my pocket."

"Good," he said. "Marvellous."

Ten minutes later we turned left off the main road into a narrow lane with high hedges on either side and from now on it was all uphill.

"How many keepers are there?" I asked.

"Three."

Claud threw away a half-finished cigarette. A minute later he lit another.

"I don't usually approve of new methods," he said. "Not on this sort of a job."

"Of course."

"But by God, Gordon, I think we're on to a hot one this time."

"You do?"

"There's no question about it."

"I hope you're right."

"It'll be a milestone in the history of poaching," he said. "But don't you go telling a single soul how we've done it, you understand. Because if this ever leaked out we'd have every bloody fool in the district doing the same thing and there wouldn't be a pheasant left."

"I won't say a word."

"You ought to be very proud of yourself," he went on. "There's been men with brains studying this problem for hundreds of years and not one of them's ever come up with anything even a quarter as artful as you have. Why didn't you tell me about it before?"

"You never invited my opinion," I said.

And that was the truth. In fact, up until the day before, Claud had never even offered to discuss with me the sacred subject of poaching. Often enough, on a summer's evening when work was finished, I had seen him with cap on head sliding quietly out of his caravan and disappearing up the road towards the woods; and sometimes, watching him through the windows of the filling-station, I would find myself wondering exactly what he was going to do, what wily tricks he was going to practise all alone up there under the trees in the dead of night. He seldom came back until very late, and never, absolutely never did he bring any of the spoils with him personally on his return. But the following afternoon – and I couldn't imagine how he did it – there would always be a pheasant or a hare or a brace of partridges hanging up in the shed behind the filling-station for us to eat.

This summer he had been particularly active, and during the last couple of months he had stepped up the tempo to a point where he was going out four and sometimes five nights a week. But that was not all. It seemed to me that recently his whole attitude towards poaching had undergone a subtle and mysterious change. He was more purposeful about it now, more tight-lipped and intense than before, and I had the impression that this was not so much a game any longer as a crusade, a sort of private war that Claud was waging single-handed against an invisible and hated enemy.

But who?

I wasn't sure about this, but I had a suspicion that it was none other than the famous Mr Victor Hazel himself, the owner of the land and the pheasants. Mr Hazel was a local brewer with an unbelievably arrogant manner. He was rich beyond words, and his property stretched for miles along either side of the valley. He was a self-made man with no charm at all and precious few virtues. He loathed all persons of humble station, having once been one of them himself, and he strove desperately to mingle with what he believed were the right kind of folk. He rode to hounds and gave shooting-parties and wore fancy waistcoats, and every weekday he drove an enormous black Rolls-Royce past the filling-station on his way to the brewery. As he flashed by, we would sometimes catch a glimpse of the great glistening brewer's face above the wheel, pink as a ham, all soft and inflamed from drinking too much beer.

Anyway, yesterday afternoon, right out of the blue, Claud had suddenly said to me, "I'll be going on up to Hazel's woods again tonight. Why don't you come along?"

"Who, me?"

"It's about the last chance this year for pheasants," he had said. "The shooting-season opens Saturday and the birds'll be scattered all over the place after that – if there's any left."

"Why the sudden invitation?" I had asked, greatly suspicious.

"No special reason, Gordon. No reason at all."

"Is it risky?"

He hadn't answered this.

"I suppose you keep a gun or something hidden away up there?"

"A gun!" he cried, disgusted. "Nobody ever *shoots* pheasants, didn't you know that? You've only got to fire a *cap-pistol* in Hazel's woods and the keepers'll be on you."

"Then how do you do it?"

"Ah," he said, and the eyelids drooped over the eyes, veiled and secretive.

There was a long pause. Then he said, "Do you think you could keep your mouth shut if I was to tell you a thing or two?"

"Definitely."

"I've never told this to anyone else in my whole life, Gordon."

"I am greatly honoured," I said. "You can trust me completely."

He turned his head, fixing me with pale eyes. The eyes were

39

large and wet and ox-like, and they were so near to me that I could see my own face reflected upside down in the centre of each.

"I am now about to let you in on the three best ways in the world of poaching a pheasant," he said. "And seeing that you're the guest on this little trip, I am going to give you the choice of which one you'd like us to use tonight. How's that?"

"There's a catch in this."

"There's no catch, Gordon. I swear it."

"All right, go on."

"Now, here's the thing," he said. "Here's the first big secret." He paused and took a long suck at his cigarette. "Pheasants," he whispered softly, "is *crazy* about raisins."

"Raisins?"

"Just ordinary raisins. It's like a mania with them. My dad discovered that more than forty years ago just like he discovered all three of these methods I'm about to describe to you now."

"I though you said your dad was a drunk."

"Maybe he was. But he was also a great poacher, Gordon. Possibly the greatest there's ever been in the history of England. My dad studied poaching like a scientist."

"Is that so?"

"I mean it. I really mean it."

"I believe you."

"Do you know," he said, "my dad used to keep a whole flock of prime cockerels in the back yard purely for experimental purposes."

"Cockerels?"

"That's right. And whenever he thought up some new stunt for catching a pheasant, he'd try it out on a cockerel first to see how it worked. That's how he discovered about raisins. It's also how he invented the horsehair method."

Claud paused and glanced over his shoulder as though to make sure that there was nobody listening. "Here's how it's done," he said. "First you take a few raisins and you soak them overnight in water to make them nice and plump and juicy. Then you get a bit of good stiff horsehair and you cut it up into half-inch lengths. Then you push one of these lengths of horse-hair through the middle of each raisin so that there's about an eighth of an inch of it sticking out on either side. You follow?"

"Yes."

"Now – the old pheasant comes along and eats one of these

raisins. Right? And you're watching him from behind a tree. So what then?"

"I imagine it sticks in his throat."

"That's obvious, Gordon. But here's the amazing thing. Here's what my dad discovered. The moment this happens, the bird *never moves his feet again*! He becomes absolutely rooted to the spot, and there he stands pumping his silly neck up and down just like it was a piston, and all you've got to do is walk calmly out from the place where you're hiding and pick him up in your hands."

"I don't believe that."

"I swear it," he said. "Once a pheasant's had the horsehair you can fire a rifle in his ear and he won't even jump. It's just one of those unexplainable little things. But it takes a genius to discover it."

He paused, and there was a gleam of pride in his eye now as he dwelt for a moment or two upon the memory of his father, the great inventor.

"So that's Method Number One," he said. "Method Number Two is even more simple still. All you do is you have a fishing line. Then you bait the hook with a raisin and you fish for the pheasant just like you fish for a fish. You pay out the line about fifty yards and you lie there on your stomach in the bushes waiting till you get a bite. Then you haul him in."

"I don't think your father invented that one."

"It's very popular with fishermen," he said, choosing not to hear me. "Keen fishermen who can't get down to the seaside as often as they want. It gives them a bit of the old thrill. The only trouble is it's rather noisy. The pheasant squawks like hell as you haul him in, and then every keeper in the wood comes running."

"What is Method Number Three?" I asked.

"Ah," he said. "Number Three's a real beauty. It was the last one my dad ever invented before he passed away."

"His final great work?"

"Exactly, Gordon. And I can even remember the very day it happened, a Sunday morning it was, and suddenly my dad comes into the kitchen holding a huge white cockerel in his hands and he says, 'I think I've got it!' There's a little smile on his face and a shine of glory in his eyes and he comes in very soft and quiet and he puts the bird down right in the middle of the kitchen table and he says, 'By God, I think I've got a good one this time!' 'A good what?' Mum says, looking up from the sink. 'Horace, take that filthy bird off my table.' The cockerel has a funny little paper hat over its head, like an ice-cream cone upside down, and my dad is pointing to it proudly. 'Stroke him,' he says. 'He won't move an inch.' The cockerel starts scratching away at the paper hat with one of its feet, but the hat seems to be stuck on with glue and it won't come off. 'No bird in the world is going to run away once you cover up his eyes,' my dad says, and he starts poking the cockerel with his finger and pushing it around on the table, but it doesn't take the slightest bit of notice. 'You can have this one,' he says, talking to Mum. 'You can kill it and dish it up for dinner as a celebration of what I have just invented.' And then straight away he takes me by the arm and marches me quickly out the door and off we go over the fields and up into the big forest the other side of Haddenham which used to belong to the Duke of Buckingham, and in less than two hours we get five lovely fat pheasants with no more trouble than it takes to go out and buy them in a shop.''

Claud paused for breath. His eyes were huge and moist and dreamy as they gazed back into the wonderful world of his youth.

"I don't quite follow this," I said. "How did he get the paper hats over the pheasants' heads up in the woods?"

"You'd never guess it."

"I'm sure I wouldn't."

"Then here it is. First of all you dig a little hole in the ground. Then you twist a piece of paper into the shape of a cone and you fit this into the hole, hollow end upward, like a cup. Then you smear the paper cup all around the inside with bird-lime and drop in a few raisins. At the same time you lay a trail of raisins along the ground leading up to it. Now – the old pheasant comes pecking along the trail, and when he gets to the hole he pops his head inside to gobble the raisins and the next thing he knows he's got a paper hat stuck over his eyes and he can't see a thing. Isn't it marvellous what some people think of, Gordon? Don't you agree?"

"Your dad was a genius," I said.

"Then take your pick. Choose whichever one of the three methods you fancy and we'll use it tonight."

"You don't think they're all just a trifle on the crude side, do you?"

"Crude!" he cried, aghast. "Oh my God! And who's been having roasted pheasant in the house nearly every single day for the last six months and not a penny to pay?"

He turned and walked away towards the door of the workshop. I could see that he was deeply pained by my remark.

"Wait a minute," I said. "Don't go."

"You want to come or don't you?"

"Yes, but let me ask you something first. I've just had a bit of an idea."

"Keep it," he said. "You are talking about a subject you don't know the first thing about."

"Do you remember that bottle of sleeping-pills the doc gave me last month when I had a bad back?"

"What about them?"

"Is there any reason why those wouldn't work on a pheasant?"

Claud closed his eyes and shook his head pityingly from side to side.

"Wait," I said.

"It's not worth discussing," he said. "No pheasant in the world is going to swallow those lousy red capsules. Don't you know any better than that?"

"You are forgetting the raisins," I said. "Now listen to this. We take a raisin. Then we soak it till it swells. Then we make a tiny slit in one side of it with a razor-blade. Then we hollow it out a little. Then we open up one of my red capsules and pour all the powder into the raisin. Then we get a needle and cotton and very carefully we sew up the slit. Now . . ."

Out of the corner of my eye, I saw Claud's mouth slowly beginning to open.

"Now," I said. "We have a nice clean-looking raisin with two and a half grains of seconal[1] inside it, and let me tell *you* something now. That's enough dope to knock the average *man* unconscious, never mind about *birds*!"

I paused for ten seconds to allow the full impact of this to strike home.

"What's more, with this method we could operate on a really grand scale. We could prepare *twenty* raisins if we felt like it, and all we'd have to do is scatter them around the feeding-grounds at sunset and then walk away. Half an hour later we'd come back, and the pills would be beginning to work, and the pheasants would be up in the trees by then, roosting, and they'd be starting to feel groggy, and they'd be wobbling and trying to keep their balance, and soon every pheasant that had eaten

---

[1] sleeping tablet

one single raisin would keel over unconscious and fall to the ground. My dear boy, they'd be dropping out of the trees like apples, and all we'd have to do is walk around picking them up!"

Claud was staring at me, rapt.

"Oh Christ," he said softly.

"And they'd never catch us either. We'd simply stroll through the woods dropping a few raisins here and there as we went, and even if they were *watching* us they wouldn't notice anything."

"Gordon," he said, laying a hand on my knee and gazing at me with eyes large and bright as two stars. "If this thing works, it will *revolutionize* poaching."

"I'm glad to hear it."

"How many pills have you got left?" he asked.

"Forty-nine. There were fifty in the bottle and I've only used one."

"Forty-nine's not enough. We want at least two hundred."

"Are you mad!" I cried.

He walked slowly away and stood by the door with his back to me, gazing at the sky.

"Two hundred's the bare minimum," he said quietly. "There's really not much point in doing it unless we have two hundred."

What is it now, I wondered. What the hell's he trying to do?

"This is the last chance we'll have before the season opens," he said.

"I couldn't possibly get any more."

"You wouldn't want us to come back empty-handed, would you?"

"But why so *many*?"

Claud turned his head and looked at me with large innocent eyes. "Why not?" he said gently. "Do you have any objection?"

My God, I thought suddenly. The crazy bastard is out to wreck Mr Victor Hazel's opening-day shooting-party.

"You get us two hundred of those pills," he said, "and then it'll be worth doing."

"I can't."

"You could try, couldn't you?"

Mr Hazel's party took place on the first of October every year and it was a very famous event. Debilitated[1] gentlemen

[1] old and feeble

in tweed suits, some with titles and some who were merely rich, motored in from miles around with their gun-bearers and dogs and wives, and all day long the noise of shooting rolled across the valley. There were always enough pheasants to go round, for each summer the woods were methodically restocked with dozens and dozens of young birds at incredible expense. I had heard it said that the cost of rearing and keeping each pheasant up to the time when it was ready to be shot was well over five pounds (which is approximately the price of two hundred loaves of bread). But to Mr Hazel it was worth every penny of it. He became, if only for a few hours, a big cheese in a little world and even the Lord Lieutenant of the County slapped him on the back and tried to remember his first name when he said good-bye.

"How would it be if we just reduced the dose?" Claud asked. "Why couldn't we divide the contents of one capsule among four raisins?"

"I suppose you could if you wanted to."

"But would a quarter of a capsule be strong enough for each bird?"

One simply had to admire the man's nerve. It was dangerous enough to poach a single pheasant up in those woods at this time of year and here he was planning to knock off the bloody lot.

"A quarter would be plenty," I said.

"You're sure of that?"

"Work it out for yourself. It's all done by bodyweight. You'd still be giving about twenty times more than is necessary."

"Then we'll quarter the dose," he said, rubbing his hands. He paused and calculated for a moment. "We'll have one hundred and ninety-six raisins!"

"Do you realize what that involves?" I said. "They'll take hours to prepare."

"What of it!" he cried. "We'll go tomorrow instead. We'll soak the raisins overnight and then we'll have all morning and afternoon to get them ready."

And that was precisely what we did.

Now, twenty-four hours later, we were on our way. We had been walking steadily for about forty minutes and we were nearing the point where the lane curved round to the right and ran along the crest of the hill towards the big wood where the pheasants lived. There was about a mile to go.

"I don't suppose by any chance these keepers might be carrying guns?" I asked.

"All keepers carry guns," Claud said.

I had been afraid of that.

"It's for the vermin mostly."

"Ah."

"Of course there's no guarantee they won't take a pot at a poacher now and again."

"You're joking."

"Not at all. But they only do it from behind. Only when you're running away. They like to pepper you in the legs at about fifty yards."

"They can't do that!" I cried. "It's a criminal offence!"

"So is poaching," Claud said.

We walked on awhile in silence. The sun was below the high hedge on our right now and the lane was in shadow.

"You can consider yourself lucky this isn't thirty years ago," he went on. "They used to shoot you on sight in those days."

"Do you believe that?"

"I know it," he said. "Many's the night when I was a nipper I've gone into the kitchen and seen my old dad lying face downward on the table and Mum standing over him digging the grapeshot out of his buttocks with a potato knife."

"Stop," I said. "It makes me nervous."

"You believe me, don't you?"

"Yes, I believe you."

"Towards the end he was so covered in tiny little white scars he looked exactly like it was snowing."

"Yes," I said. "All right."

"Poacher's arse, they used to call it," Claud said. "And there wasn't a man in the whole village who didn't have a bit of it one way or another. But my dad was the champion."

"Good luck to him," I said.

"I wish to hell he was here now," Claud said, wistful. "He'd have given anything in the world to be coming with us on this job tonight."

"He could take my place," I said. "Gladly."

We had reached the crest of the hill and now we could see the wood ahead of us, huge and dark with the sun going down behind the trees and little sparks of gold shining through.

"You'd better let me have those raisins," Claud said.

I gave him the bag and he slid it gently into his trouser pocket.

"No talking once we're inside," he said. "Just follow me and try not to go snapping any branches."

Five minutes later we were there. The lane ran right up to the wood itself and then skirted the edge of it for about three hundred yards with only a little hedge between. Claud slipped through the hedge on all fours and I followed.

It was cool and dark inside the wood. No sunlight came in at all.

"This is spooky," I said.

"Ssshh!"

Claud was very tense. He was walking just ahead of me, picking his feet up high and putting them down gently on the moist ground. He kept his head moving all the time, the eyes sweeping slowly from side to side, searching for danger. I tried doing the same, but soon I began to see a keeper behind every tree, so I gave it up.

Then a large patch of sky appeared ahead of us in the roof of the forest and I knew that this must be the clearing. Claud had told me that the clearing was the place where the young birds were introduced into the woods in early July, where they were fed and watered and guarded by the keepers, and where many of them stayed from force of habit until the shooting began.

"There's always plenty of pheasants in the clearing," he had said.

"Keepers too, I suppose."

"Yes, but there's thick bushes all around and that helps."

We were now advancing in a series of quick crouching spurts, running from tree to tree and stopping and waiting and listening and running on again, and then at last we were kneeling safely behind a big clump of alder right on the edge of the clearing and Claud was grinning and nudging me in the ribs and pointing through the branches at the pheasants.

The place was absolutely stiff with birds. There must have been two hundred of them at least strutting around among the tree-stumps.

"You see what I mean?" Claud whispered.

It was an astonishing sight, a sort of poacher's dream come true. And how close they were! Some of them were not more than ten paces from where we knelt. The hens were plump and creamy-brown and they were so fat their breast-feathers almost brushed the ground as they walked. The cocks were slim and beautiful, with long tails and brilliant red patches around the

47

eyes, like scarlet spectacles. I glanced at Claud. His big ox-like face was transfixed in ecstasy. The mouth was slightly open and the eyes had a kind of glazy look about them as they stared at the pheasants.

I believe that all poachers react in roughly the same way as this on sighting game. They are like women who sight large emeralds in a jeweller's window, the only difference being that the women are less dignified in the methods they employ later on to acquire the loot. Poacher's arse is nothing to the punishment that a female is willing to endure.

"Ah-ha," Claud said softly. "You see the keeper?"

"Where?"

"Over the other side, by that big tree. Look carefully."

"My God!"

"It's all right. He can't see *us*."

We crouched close to the ground, watching the keeper. He was a smallish man with a cap on his head and a gun under his arm. He never moved. He was like a little post standing there.

"Let's go," I whispered.

The keeper's face was shadowed by the peak of his cap, but it seemed to me that he was looking directly at us.

"I'm not staying here," I said.

"Hush," Claud said.

Slowly, never taking his eyes from the keeper, he reached into his pocket and brought out a single raisin. He placed it in the palm of his right hand, and then quickly, with a little flick of the wrist, he threw the raisin high into the air. I watched it as it went sailing over the bushes and I saw it land within a yard or so of two henbirds standing together beside an old tree-stump. Both birds turned their heads sharply at the drop of the raisin. Then one of them hopped over and made a quick peck at the ground and that must have been it.

I glanced up at the keeper. He hadn't moved.

Claud threw a second raisin into the clearing; then a third, and a fourth, and a fifth.

At this point, I saw the keeper turn away his head in order to survey the wood behind him.

Quick as a flash, Claud pulled the paper bag out of his pocket and tipped a huge pile of raisins into the cup of his right hand.

"Stop," I said.

But with a great sweep of the arm he flung the whole handful high over the bushes into the clearing.

They fell with a soft little patter, like raindrops on dry leaves, and every single pheasant in the place must either have seen them coming or heard them fall. There was a flurry of wings and a rush to find the treasure.

The keeper's head flicked round as though there were a spring inside his neck. The birds were all pecking away madly at the raisins. The keeper took two quick paces forward and for a moment I thought he was going in to investigate. But then he stopped, and his face came up and his eyes began travelling slowly around the perimeter of the clearing.

"Follow me," Claud whispered. "And *keep down*." He started crawling away swiftly on all fours, like some kind of a monkey.

I went after him. He had his nose close to the ground and his huge tight buttocks were winking at the sky and it was easy to see now how poacher's arse had come to be an occupational disease among the fraternity.[1]

We went along like this for about a hundred yards.

"Now run," Claud said.

We got to our feet and ran, and a few minutes later we emerged through the hedge into the lovely open safety of the lane.

"It went marvellous," Claud said, breathing heavily. "Didn't it go absolutely marvellous?" The big face was scarlet and glowing with triumph.

"It was a mess," I said.

"What!" he cried.

"Of course it was. We can't possibly go back now. That keeper knows there was someone there."

"He knows nothing," Claud said. "In another five minutes it'll be pitch dark inside the wood and he'll be sloping off home to his supper."

"I think I'll join him."

"You're a great poacher," Claud said. He sat down on the grassy bank under the hedge and lit a cigarette.

The sun had set now and the sky was a pale smoke blue, faintly glazed with yellow. In the woods behind us the shadows and the spaces in between the trees were turning from grey to black.

"How long does a sleeping-pill take to work?" Claud asked.

"Look out," I said, "There's someone coming."

[1] group (of poachers)

The man had appeared suddenly and silently out of the dusk and he was only thirty yards away when I saw him.

"Another bloody keeper," Claud said.

We both looked at the keeper as he came down the lane towards us. He had a shotgun under his arm and there was a black Labrador walking at his heels. He stopped when he was a few paces away and the dog stopped with him and stayed behind him, watching us through the keeper's legs.

"Good evening," Claud said, nice and friendly.

This one was a tall bony man about forty with a swift eye and a hard cheek and hard dangerous hands.

"I know you," he said softly, coming closer. "I know the both of you."

Claud didn't answer this.

"You're from the fillin'-station. Right?"

His lips were thin and dry, with some sort of a brownish crust over them.

"You're Cubbage and Hawes and you're from the fillin'-station on the main road, Right?"

"What are we playing?" Claud said. "Twenty Questions?"

The keeper spat out a big gob of spit and I saw it go floating through the air and land with a plop on a patch of dry dust six inches from Claud's feet. It looked like a little baby oyster lying there.

"Beat it," the man said. "Go on. Get out."

Claud sat on the bank smoking his cigarette and looking at the gob of spit.

"Go on," the man said. "Get out."

When he spoke, the upper lip lifted above the gum and I could see a row of small discoloured teeth, one of them black, the others quince and ochre.

"This happens to be a public highway," Claud said. "Kindly do not molest us."

The keeper shifted the gun from his left arm to his right.

"You're loiterin'," he said, "with intent to commit a felony. I could run you in for that."

"No you couldn't," Claud said.

All this made me rather nervous.

"I've had my eye on you for some time," the keeper said, looking at Claud.

"It's getting late," I said. "Shall we stroll on?"

Claud flipped away his cigarette and got slowly to his feet.

"All right," he said. "Let's go."

We wandered off down the lane the way we had come, leaving the keeper standing there, and soon the man was out of sight in the half-darkness behind us.

"That's the head keeper," Claud said. "His name is Rabbetts."

"Let's get the hell out," I said.

"Come in here," Claud said.

There was a gate on our left leading into a field and we climbed over it and sat down behind the hedge.

"Mr Rabbetts is also due for his supper," Claud said. "You mustn't worry about him."

We sat quietly behind the hedge waiting for the keeper to walk past us on his way home. A few stars were showing and a bright three-quarter moon was coming up over the hills behind us in the east.

"Here he is," Claud whispered. "Don't move."

The keeper came loping softly up the lane with the dog padding quick and soft-footed at his heels, and we watched them through the hedge as they went by.

"He won't be coming back tonight," Claud said.

"How do you know that?"

"A keeper never waits for you in the wood if he knows where you live. He goes to your house and hides outside and watches for you to come back."

"That's worse."

"No, it isn't, not if you dump the loot somewhere else before you go home. He can't touch you then."

"What about the other one, the one in the clearing?"

"He's gone too."

"You can't be sure of that."

"I've been studying these bastards for months, Gordon, honest I have. I know all their habits. There's no danger."

Reluctantly I followed him back into the wood. It was pitch dark in there now and very silent, and as we moved cautiously forward the noise of our footsteps seemed to go echoing around the walls of the forest as though we were walking in a cathedral.

"Here's where we threw the raisins," Claud said.

I peered through the bushes.

The clearing lay dim and milky in the moonlight.

"You're quite sure the keeper's gone?"

"I *know* he's gone."

I could just see Claud's face under the peak of his cap, the

51

pale lips, the soft pale cheeks, and the large eyes with a little spark of excitement dancing slowly in each.

"Are they roosting?"

"Yes."

"Whereabouts?"

"All around. They don't go far."

"What do we do next?"

"We stay here and wait. I brought you a light," he added, and he handed me one of those small pocket flashlights shaped like a fountain-pen. "You may need it."

I was beginning to feel better. "Shall we see if we can spot some of them sitting in the trees?" I said.

"No."

"I should like to see how they look when they're roosting."

"This isn't a nature-study." Claud said. "Please be quiet."

We stood there for a long time waiting for something to happen.

"I've just had a nasty thought." I said. "If a bird can keep its balance on a branch when it's asleep, then surely there isn't any reason why the pills should make it fall down."

Claud looked at me quick.

"After all," I said, "it's not dead. It's still only sleeping."

"It's doped," Claud said.

"But that's just a *deeper* sort of sleep. Why should we expect it to fall down just because it's in a *deeper* sleep?"

There was a gloomy silence.

"We should've tried it with chickens," Claud said. "My dad would've done that."

"Your dad was a genius," I said.

At that moment there came a soft thump from the wood behind us.

"Hey!"

"Ssshh!"

We stood listening.

Thump.

"There's another!"

It was a deep muffled sound as though a bag of sand had been dropped from about shoulder height.

Thump!

"They're pheasants!' I cried.

"Wait!"

"I'm sure they're pheasants!"

Thump! Thump!

"You're right!"

We ran back into the wood.

"Where were they?"

"Over here! Two of them were over here!"

"I thought they were this way."

"Keep looking!" Claud shouted. "They can't be far."

We searched for about a minute.

"Here's one!" he called.

When I got to him he was holding a magnificent cock-bird in both hands. We examined it closely with our flashlights.

"It's doped to the gills," Claud said. "It's still alive, I can feel its heart, but it's doped to the bloody gills."

Thump!

"There's another!"

Thump! Thump!

"Two more!"

Thump!

Thump! Thump! Thump!

"Jesus Christ!"

Thump! Thump! Thump! Thump!

Thump! Thump!

All around us the pheasants were starting to rain down out of the trees. We began rushing around madly in the dark, sweeping the ground with our flashlights.

Thump! Thump! Thump! This lot fell almost on top of me. I was right under the tree as they came down and I found all three of them immediately – two cocks and a hen. They were limp and warm, the feathers wonderfully soft in the hand.

"Where shall I put them?" I called out. I was holding them by the legs.

'Lay them here, Gordon! Just pile them up here where it's light!"

Claud was standing on the edge of the clearing with the moonlight streaming down all over him and a great bunch of pheasants in each hand. His face was bright, his eyes big and bright and wonderful, and he was staring around him like a child who has just discovered that the whole world is made of chocolate.

Thump!

Thump! Thump!

"I don't like it," I said. "It's too many."

"It's beautiful!" he cried and he dumped the birds he was carrying and ran off to look for more.

Thump! Thump! Thump! Thump!

Thump!

It was easy to find them now. There were one or two lying under every tree. I quickly collected six more, three in each hand, and ran back and dumped them with the others. Then six more. Then six more after that.

And still they kept falling.

Claud was in a whirl of ecstasy now, dashing about like a mad ghost under the trees. I could see the beam of his flashlight waving around in the dark and each time he found a bird he gave a little yelp of triumph.

Thump! Thump! Thump!

"That bugger Hazel ought to hear this!" he called out.

"Don't shout," I said. "It frightens me."

"What's that?"

"Don't *shout*. There might be keepers."

"Screw the keepers!" he cried. "They're all eating!"

For three or four minutes, the pheasants kept on falling. Then suddenly they stopped.

"Keep searching!" Claud shouted. "There's plenty more on the ground!"

"Don't you think we ought to get out while the going's good?"

"No," he said.

We went on searching. Between us we looked under every tree within a hundred yards of the clearing, north, south, east, and west, and I think we found most of them in the end. At the collecting-point there was a pile of pheasants as big as a bonfire.

"It's a miracle," Claud was saying. "It's a bloody miracle." He was staring at them in a kind of trance.

"We'd better just take half a dozen each and get out quick," I said.

"I would like to count them, Gordon."

"There's no time for that."

"I must count them."

"No," I said. "Come on."

"One . . .

"Two . . .

"Three . . .

"Four . . . "

He began counting them very carefully, picking up each bird in turn and laying it carefully to one side. The moon was directly overhead now and the whole clearing was brilliantly illuminated.

"I'm not standing around here like this," I said. I walked back a few paces and hid myself in the shadows, waiting for him to finish.

"A hundred and seventeen . . . a hundred and eighteen . . . a hundred and nineteen . . . *a hundred and twenty*!" he cried. "*One hundred and twenty birds*! It's an all-time record!"

I didn't doubt it for a moment.

"The most my dad ever got in one night was fifteen and he was drunk for a week afterwards!"

"You're the champion of the world," I said. "Are you ready now?"

"One minute," he answered and he pulled up his sweater and proceeded to unwind the two big white cotton sacks from around his belly. "Here's yours," he said, handing one of them to me. "Fill it up quick."

The light of the moon was so strong I could read the small print along the base of the sack. J.W. CRUMP, it said. KESTON FLOUR MILLS, LONDON SW 17.

"You don't think that bastard with the brown teeth is watching us this very moment from behind a tree?"

"There's no chance of that," Claud said. "He's down at the filling-station like I told you, waiting for us to come home."

We started loading the pheasants into the sacks. They were soft and floppy-necked and the skin underneath the feathers was still warm.

"There'll be a taxi waiting for us in the lane," Claud said.

"What?"

"I always go back in a taxi, Gordon, didn't you know that?"

I told him I didn't.

"A taxi is anonymous," Claud said. "Nobody knows who's inside a taxi except the driver. My dad taught me that."

"Which driver?"

"Charlie Kinch. He's only too glad to oblige."

We finished loading the pheasants, and I tried to hump my bulging sack on to my shoulder. My sack had about sixty birds inside it, and it must have weighed a hundredweight and a half, at least. "I can't carry this," I said. "We'll have to leave some of them behind."

"Drag it," Claud said. "Just pull it behind you."

We started off through the pitch-black woods, pulling the pheasants behind us. "We'll never make it all the way back to the village like this," I said.

"Charlie's never let me down yet," Claud said.

We came to the margin of the wood and peered through the hedge into the lane, Claud said, "Charlie boy" very softly and the old man behind the wheel of the taxi not five yards away poked his head out into the moonlight and gave us a sly toothless grin. We slid through the hedge, dragging the sacks after us along the ground.

"Hullo!" Charlie said. "What's this?"

"It's cabbages," Claud told him. "Open the door."

Two minutes later we were safely inside the taxi, cruising slowly down the hill towards the village.

It was all over now bar the shouting. Claud was triumphant, bursting with pride and excitement, and he kept leaning forward and tapping Charlie Kinch on the shoulder and saying, "How about it, Charlie? How about this for a haul?" and Charlie kept glancing back popeyed at the huge bulging sacks lying on the floor between us and saying, "Jesus Christ, man, how did you do it?"

"There's six brace of them for you, Charlie," Claud said. And Charlie said, "I reckon pheasants is going to be a bit scarce up at Mr Victor Hazel's opening-day shoot this year," and Claud said, "I imagine they are, Charlie, I imagine they are."

"What in God's name are you going to do with a hundred and twenty pheasants?" I asked.

"Put them in cold storage for the winter," Claud said. "Put them in with the dogmeat in the deep-freeze at the filling-station."

"Not tonight, I trust?"

"No, Gordon, not tonight. We leave them at Bessie's house tonight."

"Bessie who?"

"Bessie Organ."

"Bessie *Organ*!"

"Bessie always delivers my game, didn't you know that?"

"I don't know anything," I said. I was completely stunned. Mrs Organ was the wife of the Reverend Jack Organ, the local vicar.

"Always choose a respectable woman to deliver your game," Claud announced. "That's correct, Charlie, isn't it?"

"Bessie's a right smart girl," Charlie said.

We were driving through the village now and the street-lamps were still on and the men were wandering home from the pubs. I saw Will Prattley letting himself in quietly by the side-door of his fishmonger's shop and Mrs Prattley's head was sticking out of the window just above him, but he didn't know it.

"The vicar is very partial to roasted pheasant," Claud said.

"He hangs it eighteen days," Charlie said, "then he gives it a couple of good shakes and all the feathers drop off."

The taxi turned left and swung in through the gates of the vicarage. There were no lights on in the house and nobody met us. Claud and I dumped the pheasants in the coal shed at the rear, and then we said good-bye to Charlie Kinch and walked back in the moonlight to the filling-station, empty-handed. Whether or not Mr Rabbetts was watching us as we went in, I do not know. We saw no sign of him.

"Here she comes," Claud said to me the next morning.

"Who?"

"Bessie – Bessie Organ." He spoke the name proudly and with a slight proprietary air,[1] as though he were a general referring to his bravest officer.

I followed him outside.

"Down there," he said, pointing.

Far away down the road I could see a small female figure advancing towards us.

"What's she pushing?" I asked.

Claud gave me a sly look.

"There's only one safe way of delivering game," he announced, "and that's under a baby."

"Yes," I murmured, "yes, of course."

"That'll be young Christopher Organ in there, aged one and a half. He's a lovely child, Gordon."

I could just make out the small dot of a baby sitting high up in the pram, which had its hood folded down.

"There's sixty or seventy pheasants at least under that little nipper," Claud said happily. "You just imagine that."

"You can't put sixty or seventy pheasants in a pram."

"You can if it's got a good deep well underneath it, and if you take out the mattress and pack them in tight, right up to the

[1] superior, as if he owned her

57

top. All you need then is a sheet. You'll be surprised how little room a pheasant takes up when it's limp."

We stood beside the pumps waiting for Bessie Organ to arrive. It was one of those warm windless September mornings with a darkening sky and a smell of thunder in the air.

"Right through the village bold as brass," Claud said. "Good old Bessie."

"She seems in rather a hurry to me."

Claud lit a new cigarette from the stub of the old one. "Bessie is never in a hurry," he said.

"She certainly isn't walking normal," I told him. "You look."

He squinted at her through the smoke of his cigarette. Then he took the cigarette out of his mouth and looked again.

"Well?" I said.

"She does seem to be going a tiny bit quick, doesn't she?" he said carefully.

"She's going damn quick."

There was a pause. Claud was beginning to stare very hard at the approaching woman.

"Perhaps she doesn't want to be caught in the rain, Gordon. I'll bet that's exactly what it is, she thinks it's going to rain and she don't want the baby to get wet."

"Why doesn't she put the hood up?"

He didn't answer this.

"She's *running*!" I cried. "Look!" Bessie had suddenly broken into a full sprint.

Claud stood very still, watching the woman; and in the silence that followed I fancied I could hear a baby screaming.

"What's up?"

He didn't answer.

"There's something wrong with that baby," I said. "Listen."

At this point, Bessie was about two hundred yards away from us but closing fast.

"Can you hear him now?" I said.

"Yes."

"He's yelling his head off."

The small shrill voice in the distance was growing louder every second, frantic, piercing, nonstop, almost hysterical.

"He's having a fit," Claud announced.

"I think he must be."

"That's why she's running, Gordon. She wants to get him in here quick and put him under a cold tap."

"I'm sure you're right," I said. "In fact I know you're right. Just listen to that noise."

"If it isn't a fit, you can bet your life it's something like it."

"I quite agree."

Claud shifted his feet uneasily on the gravel of the driveway. "There's a thousand and one different things keep happening every day to little babies like that," he said.

"Of course."

"I knew a baby once who caught his fingers in the spokes of the pram wheel. He lost the lot. It cut them clean off."

"Yes."

"Whatever it is," Claud said, "I wish to Christ she'd stop running."

A long truck loaded with bricks came up behind Bessie and the driver slowed down and poked his head out the window to stare. Bessie ignored him and flew on, and she was so close now I could see her big red face with the mouth wide open, panting for breath. I noticed she was wearing white gloves on her hands, very prim and dainty, and there was a funny little white hat to match perched right on the top of her head, like a mushroom.

Suddenly, out of the pram, straight up into the air, flew an enormous pheasant!

Claud let out a cry of horror.

The fool in the truck going along beside Bessie started roaring with laughter.

The pheasant flapped around drunkenly for a few seconds, then it lost height and landed in the grass by the side of the road.

A grocer's van came up behind the truck and began hooting to get by. Bessie kept running.

Then – *whoosh!* – a second pheasant flew up out of the pram. Then a third, and a fourth. Then a fifth.

"My God!" I said. "It's the pills! They're wearing off!"

Claud didn't say anything.

Bessie covered the last fifty yards at a tremendous pace, and she came swinging into the driveway of the filling-station with birds flying up out of the pram in all directions.

"What the hell's going on?" she cried.

"Go round the back!" I shouted. "Go round the back!" But she pulled up sharp against the first pump in the line, and before we could reach her she had seized the screaming infant in her arms and dragged him clear.

"No! No!" Claud cried, racing towards her. "Don't lift the

baby! Put him back! Hold down the sheet!" But she wasn't even listening, and with the weight of the child suddenly lifted away, a great cloud of pheasants rose up out of the pram, fifty or sixty of them, at least, and the whole sky above us was filled with huge brown birds flapping their wings furiously to gain height.

Claud and I started running up and down the driveway waving our arms to frighten them off the premises. "Go away!" we shouted. "Shoo! Go away!" But they were too dopey still to take any notice of us and within half a minute down they came again and settled themselves like a swarm of locusts all over the front of my filling-station. The place was covered with them. They sat wing to wing along the edges of the roof and on the concrete canopy that came out over the pumps, and a dozen at least were clinging to the sill of the office window. Some had flown down on to the rack that held the bottles of lubricating-oil, and others were sliding about on the bonnets of my second-hand cars. One cockbird with a fine tail was perched superbly on top of a petrol pump, and quite a number, those that were too drunk to stay aloft, simply squatted in the driveway at our feet, fluffing their feathers and blinking their small eyes.

Across the road, a line of cars had already started forming behind the brick-lorry and the grocery-van, and people were opening their doors and getting out and beginning to cross over to have a closer look. I glanced at my watch. It was twenty to nine. Any moment now, I thought, a large black car is going to come streaking along the road from the direction of the village, and the car will be a Rolls, and the face behind the wheel will be the great glistening brewer's face of Mr Victor Hazel.

"They near pecked him to pieces!" Bessie was shouting, clasping the screaming baby to her bosom.

"You go on home, Bessie," Claud said, white in the face.

"Lock up," I said. "Put out the sign. We've gone for the day."

Galloping Foxley

Galloping Foxley

Five days a week, for thirty-six years, I have travelled the eight-twelve train to the City. It is never unduly crowded, and it takes me right in to Cannon Street Station, only an eleven and a half minute walk from the door of my office in Austin Friars.

I have always liked the process of commuting; every phase of the little journey is a pleasure to me. There is a regularity about it that is agreeable and comforting to a person of habit, and in addition, it serves as a sort of slipway along which I am gently but firmly launched into the waters of daily business routine.

Ours is a smallish country station and only nineteen or twenty people gather there to catch the eight-twelve. We are a group that rarely changes, and when occasionally a new face appears on the platform it causes a certain disclamatory, protestant[1] ripple, like a new bird in a cage of canaries.

But normally, when I arrive in the morning with my usual four minutes to spare, there they all are, these good, solid, steadfast people, standing in their right places with their right umbrellas and hats and ties and faces and their newspapers under their arms, as unchanged and unchangeable through the years as the furniture in my own living-room. I like that.

I like also my corner seat by the window and reading *The Times* to the noise and motion of the train. This part of it lasts thirty-two minutes and it seems to soothe both my brain and my fretful old body like a good long massage. Believe me, there's nothing like routine and regularity for preserving one's peace of mind. I have now made this morning journey nearly ten thousand times in all, and I enjoy it more and more every day. Also (irrelevant, but interesting), I have become a sort of clock. I can tell at once if we are running two, three, or four minutes

[1] rejecting and protesting

late, and I never have to look up to know which station we are stopped at.

The walk at the other end from Cannon Street to my office is neither too long nor too short – a healthy little perambulation[1] along streets crowded with fellow commuters all proceeding to their places of work on the same orderly schedule as myself. It gives me a sense of assurance to be moving among these dependable, dignified people who stick to their jobs and don't go gadding about all over the world. Their lives, like my own, are regulated nicely by the minute hand of an accurate watch, and very often our paths cross at the same times and places on the street each day.

For example, as I turn the corner into St Swithin's Lane, I invariably come head on with a genteel middle-aged lady who wears silver pince-nez[2] and carries a black brief-case in her hand – a first-rate accountant, I should say, or possibly an executive in the textile industry. When I cross over Threadneedle Street by the traffic lights, nine times out of ten I pass a gentleman who wears a different garden flower in his buttonhole each day. He dresses in black trousers and grey spats and is clearly a punctual and meticulous person, probably a banker, or perhaps a solicitor like myself; and several times in the last twenty-five years, as we have hurried past one another across the street, our eyes have met in a fleeting glance of mutual approval and respect.

At least half the faces I pass on this little walk are now familar to me. And good faces they are too, my kind of faces, my kind of people – sound, sedulous,[3] businesslike folk with none of that restlessness and glittering eye about them that you see in all these so-called clever types who want to tip the world upsidedown with their Labour Governments and socialized medicines and all the rest of it.

So you can see that I am, in every sense of the words, a contented commuter. Or would it be more accurate to say that I *was* a contented commuter? At the time when I wrote the little autobigraphical sketch you have just read – intending to circulate it among the staff of my office as an exhortation[4] and an example – I was giving a perfectly true account of my feelings.

---

[1] walk
[2] eye-glasses, perched on the nose
[3] diligent
[4] encouragement

But that was a whole week ago, and since then something rather peculiar has happened. As a matter of fact, it started to happen last Tuesday, the very morning that I was carrying the rough draft up to Town in my pocket; and this, to me, was so timely and coincidental that I can only believe it to have been the work of God. God had read my little essay and he had said to himself, "This man Perkins is becoming over-complacent.[1] It is high time I taught him a lesson." I honestly believe that's what happened.

As I say, it was last Tuesday, the Tuesday after Easter, a warm yellow spring morning, and I was striding on to the platform of our small country station with *The Times* tucked under my arm and the draft of "The Contented Commuter" in my pocket, when I immediately became aware that something was wrong. I could actually *feel* that curious little ripple of protest running along the ranks of my fellow commuters. I stopped and glanced around.

The stranger was standing plumb in the middle of the platform, feet apart and arms folded, looking for all the world as though he owned the whole place. He was a biggish, thickset man, and even from behind he somehow managed to convey a powerful impression of arrogance and oil. Very definitely, he was not one of us. He carried a cane instead of an umbrella, his shoes were brown instead of black, the grey hat was cocked at a ridiculous angle, and in one way and another there seemed to be an excess of silk and polish about his person. More than this I did not care to observe. I walked straight past him with my face to the sky, adding, I sincerely hope, a touch of real frost to an atmosphere that was already cool.

The train came in. And now, try if you can to imagine my horror when the new man actually followed me into *my own* compartment! Nobody had done this to me for fifteen years. My colleagues always respect my seniority. One of my special little pleasures is to have the place to myself for at least one, sometimes two or even three stations. But here, if you please, was this fellow, this stranger, straddling the seat opposite and blowing his nose and rustling the *Daily Mail* and lighting a disgusting pipe.

I lowered my *Times* and stole a glance at his face. I suppose he was about the same age as me – sixty-two or three – but he

[1] too self-satisfied

had one of those unpleasantly handsome, brown, leathery countenances that you see nowadays in advertisements for men's shirts – the lion shooter and the polo player and the Everest climber and the tropical explorer and the racing yachtsman all rolled into one; dark eyebrows, steely eyes, strong white teeth clamping the stem of a pipe. Personally, I mistrust all handsome men. The superficial pleasures of this life come too easily to them, and they seem to walk the world as though they themselves were personally responsible for their own good looks. I don't mind a *woman* being pretty. That's different. But in a man, I'm sorry, but somehow or other I find it downright offensive. Anyway, here was this one sitting right opposite me in the carriage, and I was looking at him over the top of my *Times* when suddenly he glanced up and our eyes met.

"D'you mind the pipe?" he asked, holding it up in his fingers. That was all he said. But the sound of his voice had a sudden and extraordinary effect upon me. In fact, I think I jumped. Then I sort of froze up and sat staring at him for at least a minute before I got a hold of myself and made an answer.

"This is a smoker," I said, "so you may do as you please."

"I just thought I'd ask."

There it was again, that curiously crisp, familiar voice, clipping its words and spitting them out very hard and small like a little quick-firing gun shooting out raspberry seeds. Where had I heard it before? and why did every word seem to strike upon some tiny tender spot far back in my memory? Good heavens, I thought. Pull yourself together. What sort of nonsense is this?

The stranger returned to his paper. I pretended to do the same. But by this time I was properly put out and I couldn't concentrate at all. Instead, I kept stealing glances at him over the top of the editorial page. It was really an intolerable face, vulgarly, almost lasciviously[1] handsome, with an oily salacious[2] sheen all over the skin. But had I or had I not seen it before some time in my life? I began to think I had, because now, even when I looked at it I felt a peculiar kind of discomfort that I cannot quite describe – something to do with pain and with violence, perhaps even with fear.

We spoke no more during the journey, but you can well

[1] indecently
[2] lustful

imagine that by then my whole routine had been thoroughly upset. My day was ruined; and more than one of my clerks at the office felt the sharper edge of my tongue, particularly after luncheon when my digestion started acting up on me as well.

The next morning, there he was again standing in the middle of the platform with his cane and his pipe and his silk scarf and his nauseatingly handsome face. I walked past him and approached a certain Mr Grummitt, a stockbroker who has been commuting with me for over twenty-eight years. I can't say I've ever had an actual conversation with him before – we are rather a reserved lot on our station – but a crisis like this will usually break the ice.

"Grummitt," I whispered. "Who's this bounder?"

"Search me," Grummitt said.

"Pretty unpleasant."

"Very."

"Not going to be a regular, I trust."

"Oh God," Grummitt said.

Then the train came in.

This time, to my great relief, the man got into another compartment.

But the following morning I had him with me again.

"Well," he said, settling back in the seat directly opposite. "It's a *topping* day." And once again I felt that slow uneasy stirring of the memory, stronger than ever this time, closer·to the surface but not yet quite within my reach.

Then came Friday, the last day of the week. I remember it had rained as I drove to the station, but it was one of those warm sparkling April showers that last only five or six minutes, and when I walked on to the platform, all the umbrellas were rolled up and the sun was shining and there were big white clouds floating in the sky. In spite of this, I felt depressed. There was no pleasure in this journey for me any longer. I knew the stranger would be there. And sure enough, he was, standing with his legs apart just as though he owned the place, and this time swinging his cane casually back and forth through the air.

The cane! That did it! I stopped like I'd been shot.

"It's Foxley!" I cried under my breath. "Galloping Foxley! And still swinging his cane!"

I stepped closer to get a better look. I tell you I've never had such a shock in all my life. It was Foxley all right. Bruce Foxley or Galloping Foxley as we used to call him. And the last time

I'd seen him, let me see – it was at school and I was no more than twelve or thirteen years old.

At that point the train came in, and heaven help me if he didn't get into my compartment once again. He put his hat and cane up on the rack, then turned and sat down and began lighting his pipe. He glanced up at me through the smoke with those rather small cold eyes and he said, "*Ripping* day, isn't it. Just like summer."

There was no mistaking the voice now. It hadn't changed at all. Except that the things I had been used to hearing it say were different.

"All right, Perkins," it used to say. "All right, you nasty little boy. I am about to beat you again."

How long ago was that? It must be nearly fifty years. Extra-ordinary, though, how little the features had altered. Still the same arrogant tilt of the chin, the flaring nostrils, the con-temptuous staring eyes that were too small and a shade too close together for comfort; still the same habit of thrusting his face forward at you, impinging on[1] you, pushing you into a corner; and even the hair I could remember – coarse and slightly wavy, with just a trace of oil all over it, like a well-tossed salad. He used to keep a bottle of green hair mixture on the side table in his study – when you have to dust a room you get to know and to hate all the objects in it – and this bottle had the royal coat of arms on the label and the name of a shop in Bond Street, and under that, in small print, it said "By Appointment – Hairdressers To His Majesty King Edward VII." I can remember that particularly because it seemed so funny that a shop should want to boast about being hairdresser to someone who was practically bald – even a monarch.

And now I watched Foxley settle back in his seat and begin reading the paper. It was a curious sensation, sitting only a yard away from this man who fifty years before had made me so miserable that I had once contemplated suicide. He hadn't recognized *me*; there wasn't much danger of that because of my moustache. I felt fairly sure I was safe and could sit there and watch him all I wanted.

Looking back on it, there seems little doubt that I suffered very badly at the hands of Bruce Foxley my first year in school, and strangely enough, the unwitting cause of it all was my

[1] striking at

father. I was twelve and a half when I first went off to this fine
old public school. That was, let me see, in 1907. My father,
who wore a silk topper and morning coat, escorted me to the
station, and I can remember how we were standing on the platform among piles of wooden tuck-boxes and trunks and what
seemed like thousands of very large boys milling about and
talking and shouting at one another, when suddenly somebody
who was wanting to get by us gave my father a great push from
behind and nearly knocked him off his feet.

My father, who was a small, courteous, dignified person,
turned around with surprising speed and seized the culprit by
the wrist.

"Don't they teach you better manners than that at this
school, young man?" he said.

The boy, at least a head taller than my father, looked down
at him with a cold, arrogant-laughing glare, and said nothing.

"It seems to me," my father said, staring back at him, "that
an apology would be in order."

But the boy just kept on looking down his nose at my father
with this funny little arrogant smile at the corners of his mouth,
and his chin kept coming further and further out.

"You strike me as being an impudent and ill-mannered boy,"
my father went on. "And I can only pray that you are an
exception in your school. I would not wish for any son of mine
to pick up such habits."

At this point, the big boy inclined his head slightly in my
direction, and a pair of small, cold, rather close together eyes
looked down into mine. I was not particularly frightened at the
time; I knew nothing about the power of senior boys over
junior boys at public schools; and I can remember that I looked
straight back at him in support of my father, whom I adored
and respected.

When my father started to say something more, the boy
simply turned away and sauntered slowly down the platform
into the crowd.

Bruce Foxley never forgot this episode; and of course the
really unlucky thing about it for me was that when I arrived
at school I found myself in the same "house" as him. Even
worse than that – I was in his study. He was doing his last year,
and he was a prefect – "a boazer" we called it – and as such he
was officially permitted to beat any of the fags in the house. But
being in his study, I automatically became his own particular,

personal slave. I was his valet and cook and maid and errand-boy, and it was my duty to see that he never lifted a finger for himself unless absolutely necessary. In no society that I know of in the world is a servant imposed upon to the extent that we wretched little fags were imposed upon by the boazers at school. In frosty or snowy weather I even had to sit on the seat of the lavatory (which was in an unheated outhouse) every morning after breakfast to warm it before Foxley came along.

I could remember how he used to saunter across the room in his loose-jointed, elegant way, and if a chair were in his path he would knock it aside and I would have to run over and pick it up. He wore silk shirts and always had a silk handkerchief tucked up his sleeve, and his shoes were made by someone called Lobb (who also had a royal crest). They were pointed shoes, and it was my duty to rub the leather with a bone for fifteen minutes each day to make it shine.

But the worst memories of all had to do with the changing-room.

I could see myself now, a small pale shrimp of a boy standing just inside the door of this huge room in my pyjamas and bed-room slippers and brown camel-hair dressing-gown. A single bright electric bulb was hanging on a flex from the ceiling, and all around the walls the black and yellow football shirts with their sweaty smell filling the room, and the voice, the clipped, pip-spitting voice was saying. "So which is it to be this time? Six with the dressing gown on – or four with it off?"

I never could bring myself to answer this question. I would simply stand there staring down at the dirty floor-planks, dizzy with fear and unable to think of anything except that this other larger boy would soon start smashing away at me with his long, thin, white stick, slowly, scientifically, skilfully, legally, and with apparent relish, and I would bleed. Five hours earlier, I had failed to get the fire to light in his study. I had spent my pocket money on a box of special firelighters and I had held a news-paper across the chimney opening to make a draught and I had knelt down in front of it and blown my guts out into the bottom of the grate; but the coals would not burn.

"If you're too obstinate to answer," the voice was saying, "then I'll have to decide for you."

I wanted desperately to answer because I knew which one I had to choose. It's the first thing you learn when you arrive. Always keep the dressing-gown *on* and take the extra strokes.

Otherwise you're almost certain to get cut. Even three with it on is better than one with it off.

"Take it off then and get into the far corner and touch your toes. I'm going to give you four."

Slowly I would take it off and lay it on the ledge above the boot-lockers. And slowly I would walk over to the far corner, cold and naked now in my cotton pyjamas, treading softly and seeing everything around me suddenly very bright and flat and far away, like a magic lantern picture, and very big, and very unreal, and sort of swimming through the water in my eyes.

"Go on and touch your toes. Tighter – much tighter than that."

Then he would walk down to the far end of the changing-room and I would be watching him upside down between my legs, and he would disappear through a doorway that led down two steps into what we called "the basin-passage". This was a stone-floored corridor with wash basins along one wall, and beyond it was the bathroom. When Foxley disappeared I knew he was walking down to the far end of the basin-passage. Foxley always did that. Then, in the distance, but echoing loud among the basins and the tiles, I would hear the noise of his shoes on the stone floor as he started galloping forward, and through my legs I would see him leaping up the two steps into the changing-room and come bounding towards me with his face thrust forward and the cane held high in the air. This was the moment when I shut my eyes and waited for the crack and told myself that whatever happened I must not straighten up.

Anyone who has been properly beaten will tell you that the real pain does not come until about eight or ten seconds after the stroke. The stroke itself is merely a loud crack and a sort of blunt thud against your backside, numbing you completely (I'm told a bullet wound does the same). But later on, oh my heavens, if feels as if someone is laying a red hot poker right across your naked buttocks and it is absolutely impossible to prevent yourself from reaching back and clutching it with your fingers.

Foxley knew all about this time lag, and the slow walk back over a distance that must altogether have been fifteen yards gave each stroke plenty of time to reach the peak of its pain before the next one was delivered.

On the fourth stroke I would invariably straighten up. I couldn't help it. It was an automatic defence reaction from a body that had had as much as it could stand.

"You flinched," Foxley would say. "That one doesn't count. Go on – down you get."

The next time I would remember to grip my ankles.

Afterwards he would watch me as I walked over – very stiff now and holding my backside – to put on my dressing-gown, but I would always try to keep turned away from him so he couldn't see my face. And when I went out, it would be, "Hey, you! Come back!"

I was in the passage then, and I would stop and turn and stand in the doorway, waiting.

"Come here. Come on, come back here. Now – haven't you forgotten something?"

All I could think of at that moment was the excruciating[1] burning pain in my behind.

"You strike me as being an impudent and ill-mannered boy," he would say, imitating my father's voice. "Don't they teach you better manners than that at this school?"

"Thank . . . you," I would stammer. "Thank . . . you . . . for the beating."

And then back up the dark stairs to the dormitory and it became much better then because it was all over and the pain was going and the others were clustering round and treating me with a certain rough sympathy born of having gone through the same thing themselves, many times.

"Hey, Perkins, let's have a look."

"How many d'you get?"

"Five, wasn't it? We heard them easily from here."

"Come on, man. Let's see the marks."

I would take down my pyjamas and stand there while this group of experts solemnly examined the damage.

"Rather far apart, aren't they? Not quite up to Foxley's usual standard."

"Two of them are close. Actually touching. Look – these two are beauties!"

"That low one was a rotten shot."

"Did he go right down the basin-passage to start his run?"

"You got an extra one for flinching, didn't you?"

"By golly, old Foxley's really got it in for *you*, Perkins."

"Bleeding a bit too. Better wash it, you know."

[1] extremely painful

Then the door would open and Foxley would be there, and everyone would scatter and pretend to be doing his teeth or saying his prayers while I was left standing in the centre of the room with my pants down.

"What's going on here?" Foxley would say, taking a quick look at his own handiwork. "You – Perkins! Put your pyjamas on properly and get into bed."

And that was the end of a day.

Through the week, I never had a moment of time to myself. If Foxley saw me in the study taking up a novel or perhaps opening my stamp album, he would immediately find something for me to do. One of his favourites, especially when it was raining outside, was "Oh, Perkins, I think a bunch of wild irises would look rather nice on my desk, don't you?"

Wild irises grew only around Orange Ponds. Orange Ponds was two miles down the road and half a mile across the fields. I would get up from my chair, put on my raincoat and my straw hat, take my umbrella – my brolly – and set off on this long and lonely trek. The straw hat had to be worn at all times outdoors, but it was easily destroyed by rain; therefore the brolly was necessary to protect the hat. On the other hand, you can't keep a brolly over your head while scrambling about on a woody bank looking for irises, so to save my hat from ruin I would put it on the ground under my brolly while I searched for flowers. In this way, I caught many colds.

But the most dreaded day was Sunday. Sunday was for cleaning the study, and how well I can remember the terror of those mornings, the frantic dusting and scrubbing, and then the waiting for Foxley to come in to inspect.

"Finished?" he would ask.

"I . . . I think so."

Then he would stroll over to the drawer of his desk and take out a single white glove, fitting it slowly on to his right hand, pushing each finger well home, and I would stand there watching and trembling as he moved around the room running his white gloved forefinger along the picture tops, the skirting, the shelves, the window sills, the lamp shades. I never took my eyes off that finger. For me it was an instrument of doom. Nearly always, it managed to discover some tiny crack that I had overlooked or perhaps hadn't even thought about; and when this happened Foxley would turn slowly around, smiling that dangerous little smile that wasn't a smile, holding up the white finger so that I should see for myself the thin smudge of dust that lay along the side of it.

"Well," he would say. "So you're a lazy little boy. Aren't you?"

No answer.

"Aren't you?"

"I thought I dusted it all."

"Are you or are you not a nasty, lazy little boy?"

"Y-yes."

"But your father wouldn't want you to grow up like that, would he? Your father is very particular about manners, is he not?"

No answer.

"I asked you, is your father particular about manners?"

"Perhaps – yes."

"Therefore I will be doing him a favour if I punish you, won't I?"

"I don't know."

"Won't I?"

"Y-yes?"

"We will meet later then, after prayers, in the changing-room."

The rest of the day would be spent in an agony of waiting for the evening to come.

Oh my goodness, how it was all coming back to me now. Sunday was also letter-writing time. "Dear Mummy and Daddy – thank you very much for your letter. I hope you are both well. I am, except I have got a cold because I got caught in the rain but it will soon be over. Yesterday we played Shrewsbury and beat them 4–2. I watched and Foxley who you know is the head of our house scored one of our goals. Thank you very much for the cake. With love from William."

I usually went to the lavatory to write my letter, or to the boot-hole, or the bathroom – any place out of Foxley's way. But I had to watch the time. Tea was at four-thirty and Foxley's toast had to be ready. Every day I had to make toast for Foxley, and on weekdays there were no fires allowed in the studies, so all the fags, each making toast for his own studyholder, would have to crowd around the one small fire in the library, jockeying for position with his toasting-fork. Under these conditions, I still had to see that Foxley's toast was (1) very crisp, (2) not burned at all, (3) hot and ready exactly on time. To fail in any one of these requirements was a "beatable offence".

"Hey, you! What's this?"

"It's toast."

"Is this really your idea of toast?"

"Well . . ."

"You're too idle to make it right, aren't you?"

"I try to make it."

"You know what they do to an idle horse, Perkins?"

"No,"

"Are you a horse?"

"No."

"Well – anyway, you're an ass – ha, ha – so I think you qualify. I'll be seeing you later."

Oh, the agony of those days. To burn Foxley's toast was a "beatable offence". So was forgetting to take the mud off Foxley's football boots. So was failing to hang up Foxley's football clothes. So was rolling up Foxley's brolly the wrong way round. So was banging the study door when Foxley was working. So was filling Foxley's bath too hot for him. So was not cleaning the buttons properly on Foxley's O.T.C. uniform. So was making those blue metal-polish smudges on the uniform itself. So was failing to shine the *soles* of Foxley's shoes. So was leaving Foxley's study untidy at any time. In fact, so far as Foxley was concerned, I was practically a beatable offence myself.

I glanced out of the window. My goodness, we were nearly there. I must have been dreaming away like this for quite a while, and I hadn't even opened my *Times*. Foxley was still leaning back in the corner seat opposite me reading his *Daily Mail*, and through a cloud of blue smoke from his pipe I could see the top half of his face over the newspaper, the small bright eyes, the corrugated forehead, the wavy, slightly oily hair.

Looking at him now, after all that time, was a peculiar and rather exciting experience. I knew he was no longer dangerous, but the old memories were still there and I didn't feel altogether comfortable in his presence. It was something like being inside the cage with a tame tiger.

What nonsense is this? I asked myself. Don't be so stupid. My heavens, if you wanted to you could go ahead and tell him exactly what you thought of him and he couldn't touch you. Hey – that was an idea!

Except that – well – after all, was it worth it? I was too old for that sort of thing now, and I wasn't sure that I really felt much anger towards him anyway.

So what should I do? I couldn't sit there staring at him like an idiot.

At that point, a little impish fancy began to take a hold of me. What I would like to do, I told myself, would be to lean across and tap him lightly on the knee and tell him who I was. Then I would watch his face. After that, I would begin talking about our schooldays together, making it just loud enough for the other people in the carriage to hear. I would remind him playfully of some of the things he used to do to me, and perhaps even describe the changing-room beatings so as to embarrass him a trifle. A bit of teasing and discomfort wouldn't do him any harm. And it would do *me* an awful lot of good.

Suddenly he glanced up and caught me staring at him. It was the second time this had happened, and I noticed a flicker of irritation in his eyes.

All right, I told myself. Here we go. But keep it pleasant and sociable and polite. It'll be much more effective that way, more embarrassing for him.

So I smiled at him and gave him a courteous little nod. Then, raising my voice, I said, "I do hope you'll excuse me. I'd like to introduce myself." I was leaning forward watching him closely so as not to miss the reaction. "My name is Perkins – William Perkins – and I was at Repton in 1907."

The others in the carriage were sitting very still, and I could sense that they were all listening and waiting to see what would happen next.

"I'm glad to meet you," he said, lowering the paper to his lap. "Mine's Fortescue – Jocelyn Fortescue. Eton, 1916."

Mrs Bixby and the Colonel's Coat

Mrs Bixby and the Colonel's Coat

America is the land of opportunities for women. Already they own about eighty-five per cent of the wealth of the nation. Soon they will have it all. Divorce has become a lucrative[1] process, simple to arrange and easy to forget; and ambitious females can repeat it as often as they please and parlay their winnings to astronomical figures. The husband's death also brings satisfactory rewards and some ladies prefer to rely upon this method. They know that the waiting period will not be unduly protracted, for overwork and hypertension are bound to get the poor devil before long, and he will die at his desk with a bottle of benzedrines[2] in one hand and a packet of tranquillizers in the other.

Succeeding generations of youthful American males are not deterred in the slightest by this terrifying pattern of divorce and death. The higher the divorce rate climbs, the more eager they become. Young men marry like mice, almost before they have reached the age of puberty, and a large proportion of them have at least two ex-wives on the payroll by the time they are thirty-six years old. To support these ladies in the manner to which they are accustomed, the men must work like slaves, which is of course precisely what they are. But now at last, as they approach their premature middle age, a sense of disillusionment and fear begins to creep slowly into their hearts, and in the evenings they take to huddling together in little groups, in clubs and bars, drinking their whiskies and swallowing their pills, and trying to comfort one another with stories.

The basic theme of these stories never varies. There are always three main characters – the husband, the wife, and the dirty dog. The husband is a decent clean-living man, working hard at his job. The wife is cunning, deceitful, and lecherous, and she is invariably up to some sort of jiggery-pokery with the dirty dog. The husband is too good a man even to suspect her. Things

[1] profitable
[2] energy-giving pills

look black for the husband. Will the poor man ever find out? Must he be a cuckold[1] for the rest of his life? Yes, he must. But wait! Suddenly, by a brilliant manoeuvre, the husband completely turns the tables on his monstrous spouse. The woman is flabbergasted, stupefied, humiliated, defeated. The audience of men around the bar smiles quietly to itself and takes a little comfort from the fantasy.

There are many of these stories going around, these wonderful wishful-thinking dreamworld inventions of the unhappy male, but most of them are too fatuous to be worth repeating, and far too fruity to be put down on paper. There is one, however, that seems to be superior to the rest, particularly as it has the merit of being true. It is extremely popular with twice- or thrice-bitten males in search of solace, and if you are one of them, and if you haven't heard it before, you may enjoy the way it comes out. The story is called "Mrs Bixby and the Colonel's Coat", and it goes something like this:

Mr and Mrs Bixby lived in a smallish apartment somewhere in New York City. Mr Bixby was a dentist who made an average income. Mrs Bixby was a big vigorous woman with a wet mouth. Once a month, always on Friday afternoons, Mrs Bixby would board the train at Pennsylvania Station and travel to Baltimore to visit her old aunt. She would spend the night with the aunt and return to New York on the following day in time to cook supper for her husband. Mr Bixby accepted this arrangement goodnaturedly. He knew that Aunt Maude lived in Baltimore, and that his wife was very fond of the old lady, and certainly it would be unreasonable to deny either of them the pleasure of a monthly meeting.

"Just so long as you don't ever expect me to accompany you," Mr Bixby had said in the beginning.

"Of course not, darling," Mrs Bixby had answered. "After all, she is not *your* aunt. She's mine."

So far so good.

As it turned out, however, the aunt was little more than a convenient alibi for Mrs Bixby. The dirty dog, in the shape of a gentleman known as the Colonel, was lurking slyly in the background, and our heroine spent the greater part of her Baltimore time in this scoundrel's company. The Colonel was exceedingly wealthy. He lived in a charming house on the

[1] a man whose wife has been unfaithful

79

outskirts of the town. No wife or family encumbered him, only a few discreet and loyal servants, and in Mrs Bixby's absence he consoled himself by riding his horses and hunting the fox.

Year after year, this pleasant alliance between Mrs Bixby and the Colonel continued without a hitch. They met so seldom – twelve times a year is not much when you come to think of it – that there was little or no chance of their growing bored with one another. On the contrary, the long wait between meetings only made the heart grow fonder, and each separate occasion became an exciting reunion.

"Tally-ho!" the Colonel would cry each time he met her at the station in the big car. "My dear, I'd almost forgotten how ravishing you looked. Let's go to earth."

Eight years went by.

It was just before Christmas, and Mrs Bixby was standing on the station in Baltimore waiting for the train to take her back to New York. This particular visit which had just ended had been more than usually agreeable, and she was in a cheerful mood. But then the Colonel's company always did that to her these days. The man had a way of making her feel that she was altogether a rather remarkable woman, a person of subtle and exotic talents, fascinating beyond measure; and what a very different thing that was from the dentist husband at home who never succeeded in making her feel that she was anything but a sort of eternal patient, someone who dwelt in the waiting-room, silent among the magazines, seldom if ever nowadays to be called in to suffer the finicky precise ministrations[1] of those clean pink hands.

"The Colonel asked me to give you this," a voice beside her said. She turned and saw Wilkins, the Colonel's groom, a small wizened dwarf with grey skin, and he was pushing a large flattish cardboard box into her arms.

"Good gracious me!" she cried, all of a flutter. "My heavens, what an enormous box! What is it, Wilkins? Was there a message? Did he send me a message?"

"No message," the groom said, and he walked away.

As soon as she was on the train, Mrs Bixby carried the box into the privacy of the Ladies' Room and locked the door. How exciting this was! A Christmas present from the Colonel. She started to undo the string. "I'll bet it's a dress," she said

[1] attentions

aloud. "It might even be two dresses. Or it might be a whole lot of beautiful underclothes. I won't look. I'll just feel around and try to guess what it is. I'll try to guess the colour as well, and exactly what it looks like. Also how much it cost."

She shut her eyes tight and slowly lifted off the lid. Then she put one hand down into the box. There was some tissue paper on top; she could feel it and hear it rustling. There was also an envelope or a card of some sort. She ignored this and began burrowing underneath the tissue paper, the fingers reaching out delicately, like tendrils.

"My God," she cried suddenly. "It can't be true!"

She opened her eyes wide and stared at the coat. Then she pounced on it and lifted it out of the box. Thick layers of fur made a lovely noise against the tissue paper as they unfolded, and when she held it up and saw it hanging to its full length, it was so beautiful it took her breath away.

Never had she seen mink like this before. It *was* mink, wasn't it? Yes, of course it was. But what a glorious colour! The fur was almost pure black. At first she thought it *was* black; but when she held it closer to the window she saw that there was a touch of blue in it as well, a deep rich blue, like cobalt. Quickly she looked at the label. It said simply, WILD LABRADOR MINK. There was nothing else, no sign of where it had been bought or anything. But that, she told herself, was probably the Colonel's doing. The wily old fox was making darn sure he didn't leave any tracks. Good for him. But what in the world could it have cost? She hardly dared to think. Four, five six thousand dollars? Possibly more.

She just couldn't take her eyes off it. Nor, for that matter, could she wait to try it on. Quickly she slipped off her own plain red coat. She was panting a little now, she couldn't help it, and her eyes were stretched very wide. But oh God, the feel of that fur! And those huge wide sleeves with their thick turned-up cuffs! Who was it had once told her that they always used female skins for the arms and male skins for the rest of the coat? Someone had told her that. Joan Rutfield, probably; though how *Joan* would know anything about *mink* she couldn't imagine.

The great black coat seemed to slide on to her almost of its own accord, like a second skin. Oh boy! It was the queerest feeling! She glanced into the mirror. It was fantastic. Her whole personality had suddenly changed completely. She looked dazzling, radiant, rich, brilliant, voluptuous, all at the same time.

And the sense of power that it gave her! In this coat she could walk into any place she wanted and people would come scurrying around her like rabbits. The whole thing was just too wonderful for words!

Mrs Bixby picked up the envelope that was still lying in the box. She opened it and pulled out the Colonel's letter:

> I once heard you saying you were fond of mink so I got you this. I'm told it's a good one. Please accept it with my sincere good wishes as a parting gift. For my own personal reasons I shall not be able to see you any more. Good-bye and good luck.

Well!

Imagine that!

Right out of the blue, just when she was feeling so happy.

No more Colonel.

What a dreadful shock.

She would miss him enormously.

Slowly, Mrs Bixby began stroking the lovely soft black fur of the coat.

What you lose on the swings you get back on the roundabouts.

She smiled and folded the letter, meaning to tear it up and throw it out of the window, but in folding it she noticed that there was something written on the other side:

P.S. just tell them that nice generous aunt of yours gave it to you for Christmas.

Mrs Bixby's mouth, at that moment stretched wide in a silky smile, snapped back like a piece of elastic.

"The man must be mad!" she cried. "Aunt Maude doesn't have that sort of money. She couldn't possibly give me this."

But if Aunt Maude didn't give it to her, then who did?

Oh God! In the excitement of finding the coat and trying it on, she had completely overlooked this vital aspect.

In a couple of hours she would be in New York. Ten minutes after that she would be home, and the husband would be there to greet her; and even a man like Cyril, dwelling as he did in a dark phlegmy world of root canals, bicuspids, and caries,[1] would start asking a few questions if his wife suddenly waltzed in from a week-end wearing a six-thousand-dollar mink coat.

You know what I think, she told herself. I think that god-

---

[1] technical dental words

damn Colonel has done this on purpose just to torture me. He knew perfectly well Aunt Maude didn't have enough money to buy this. He knew I wouldn't be able to keep it.

But the thought of parting with it now was more than Mrs Bixby could bear.

"I've *got* to have this coat!" she said aloud. "I've got to have this coat! I've got to have this coat!"

Very well, my dear. You shall have the coat. But don't panic. Sit still and keep calm and start thinking. You're a clever girl, aren't you? You've fooled him before. The man never has been able to see much further than the end of his own probe, you know that. So just sit absolutely still and *think*. There's lots of time.

Two and a half hours later, Mrs Bixby stepped off the train at Pennsylvania Station and walked quickly to the exit. She was wearing her old red coat again now and carrying the cardboard box in her arms. She signalled for a taxi.

"Driver," she said, "would you know of a pawnbroker that's still open around here?"

The man behind the wheel raised his brows and looked back at her, amused.

"Plenty along Sixth Avenue," he answered.

"Stop at the first one you see, then, will you please?" She got in and was driven away.

Soon the taxi pulled up outside a shop that had three brass balls hanging over the entrance.

"Wait for me, please," Mrs Bixby said to the driver, and she got out of the taxi and entered the shop.

There was an enormous cat crouching on the counter eating fishheads out of a white saucer. The animal looked up at Mrs Bixby with bright yellow eyes, then looked away again and went on eating. Mrs Bixby stood by the counter, as far away from the cat as possible, waiting for someone to come, staring at the watches, the shoe buckles, the enamel brooches, the old binoculars, the broken spectacles, the false teeth. Why did they always pawn their teeth, she wondered.

"Yes?" the proprietor said, emerging from a dark place in the back of the shop.

"Oh, good evening," Mrs Bixby said. She began to untie the string around the box. The man went up to the cat and started stroking it along the top of its back, and the cat went on eating the fishheads.

"Isn't it silly of me?" Mrs Bixby said. "I've gone and lost my pocketbook, and this being Saturday, the banks are all closed until Monday and I've simply got to have some money for the week-end. This is quite a valuable coat, but I'm not asking much. I only want to borrow enough on it to tide me over till Monday. Then I'll come back and redeem it."

The man waited, and said nothing. But when she pulled out the mink and allowed the beautiful thick fur to fall over the counter, his eyebrows went up and he drew his hand away from the cat and came over to look at it. He picked it up and held it out in front of him.

"If only I had a watch on me or a ring," Mrs Bixby said, "I'd give you that instead. But the fact is I don't have a thing with me other than this coat." She spread out her fingers for him to see.

"It looks new," the man said, fondling the soft fur.

"Oh yes, it is. But, as I said, I only want to borrow enough to tide me over till Monday. How about fifty dollars?"

"I'll loan you fifty dollars."

"It's worth a hundred times more than that, but I know you'll take good care of it until I return."

The man went over to a drawer and fetched a ticket and placed it on the counter. The ticket looked like one of those labels you tie on to the handle of your suitcase, the same shape and size exactly, and the same stiff brownish paper. But it was perforated across the middle so that you could tear it in two, and both halves were identical.

"Name?" he asked.

"Leave that out. And the address."

She saw the man pause, and she saw the nib of the pen hovering over the dotted line, waiting.

"You don't *have* to put the name and address, do you?"

The man shrugged and shook his head and the pen-nib moved on down to the next line.

"It's just that I'd rather not," Mrs Bixby said. "It's purely personal."

"You'd better not lose this ticket, then."

"I won't lose it."

"You realize that anyone who gets hold of it can come in and claim the article?"

"Yes, I know that."

"Simply on the number."

"Yes, I know."

"What do you want me to put for a description."

"No description either, thank you. It's not necessary. Just put the amount I'm borrowing."

The pen-nib hesitated again, hovering over the dotted line beside the word ARTICLE.

"I think you ought to put a description. A description is always a help if you want to sell the ticket. You never know, you might want to sell it sometime."

"I don't want to sell it."

"You might have to. Lots of people do."

"Look," Mrs Bixby said. "I'm not broke, if that's what you mean. I simply lost my purse. Don't you understand?"

"You have it your own way then," the man said. "It's your coat."

At this point an unpleasant thought struck Mrs Bixby. "Tell me something," she said. "If I don't have a description on my ticket, how can I be sure you'll give me back the coat and not something else when I return?"

"It goes in the books."

"But all I've got is a number. So actually you could hand me any old thing you wanted, isn't that so?"

"Do you want a description or don't you?" the man asked.

"No," she said. "I trust you."

The man wrote "fifty dollars" opposite the word VALUE on both sections of the ticket, then he tore it in half along the perforations and slid the lower portion across the counter. He took a wallet from the inside pocket of his jacket and extracted five ten-dollar bills. "The interest is three per cent a month," he said.

"Yes, all right. And thank you. You'll take good care of it, won't you?"

The man nodded but said nothing.

"Shall I put it back in the box for you?"

"No," the man said.

Mrs Bixby turned and went out of the shop on to the street where the taxi was waiting. Ten minutes later, she was home.

"Darling," she said as she bent over and kissed her husband. "Did you miss me?"

Cyril Bixby laid down the evening paper and glanced at the watch on his wrist. "It's twelve and a half minutes past six," he said. "You're a bit late, aren't you?"

"I know. It's those dreadful trains. Aunt Maude sent you her love as usual. I'm dying for a drink, aren't you?"

The husband folded his newspaper into a neat rectangle and placed it on the arm of his chair. Then he stood up and crossed over to the sideboard. His wife remained in the centre of the room pulling off her gloves, watching him carefully, wondering how long she ought to wait. He had his back to her now, bending forward to measure the gin, putting his face right up close to the measurer and peering into it as though it were a patient's mouth.

It was funny how small he always looked after the Colonel. The Colonel was huge and bristly, and when you were near to him he smelled faintly of horseradish. This one was small and neat and bony and he didn't really smell of anything at all, except peppermint drops, which he sucked to keep his breath nice for the patients.

"See what I've brought for measuring the vermouth," he said, holding up a calibrated glass beaker. "I can get it to the nearest milligram with this."

"Darling, how clever."

I really must try to make him change the way he dresses, she told herself. His suits are just too ridiculous for words. There had been a time when she thought they were wonderful, those Edwardian jackets with high lapels and six buttons down the front, but now they merely seemed absurd. So did the narrow stovepipe trousers. You had to have a special sort of face to wear things like that, and Cyril just didn't have it. His was a long bony countenance with a narrow nose and a slightly prognathous[1] jaw, and when you saw it coming up out of the top of one of those tightly fitting old-fashioned suits it looked like a caricature of Sam Weller.[2] He probably thought it looked like Beau Brummel.[3] It was a fact that in the office he invariably greeted female patients with his white coat unbuttoned so that they would catch a glimpse of the trappings underneath; and in some obscure way this was obviously meant to convey the impression that he was a bit of a dog. But Mrs Bixby knew better. The plumage was a bluff. It meant nothing. It reminded her of an ageing peacock strutting on the lawn with only half its feathers left. Or one of those fatuous self-fertilizing flowers – like the dandelion.

[1] projecting
[2] one of Charles Dickens's characters
[3] a famous early nineteenth century man of fashion

A dandelion never has to get fertilized for the setting of its seed, and all those brilliant yellow petals are just a waste of time, a boast, a masquerade. What's the word the biologists use? Subsexual. A dandelion is subsexual. So, for that matter, are the summer broods of water fleas. It sounds a bit like Lewis Carroll, she thought – water fleas and dandelions and dentists.

"Thank you, darling,". she said, taking the martini and seating herself on the sofa with her handbag on her lap. "And what did *you* do last night?"

"I stayed on in the office and cast a few inlays.[1] I also got my accounts up to date."

"Now really, Cyril, I think it's high time you let other people do your donkey work for you. You're much too important for that sort of thing. Why don't you give the inlays to the mechanic?"

"I prefer to do them myself. I'm extremely proud of my inlays."

"I know you are, darling, and I think they're absolutely wonderful. They're the best inlays in the whole world. But I don't want you to burn yourself out. And why doesn't that Pulteney woman do the accounts? That's part of her job, isn't it?"

"She does do them. But I have to price everything up first. She doesn't know who's rich and who isn't."

"This Martini is perfect," Mrs Bixby said, setting down her glass on the side table. "Quite perfect." She opened her bag and took out a handkerchief as if to blow her nose. "Oh look!" she cried, seeing the ticket. "I forgot to show you this! I found it just now on the seat of my taxi. It's got a number on it, and I thought it might be a lottery ticket or something, so I kept it."

She handed the small piece of stiff brown paper to her husband, who took it in his fingers and began examining it minutely from all angles, as though it were a suspect tooth.

"You know what this is?" he said slowly.

"No dear, I don't."

"It's a pawn ticket."

"A what?"

"A ticket from a pawnbroker. Here's the name and address of the shop – somewhere on Sixth Avenue."

[1] gold fillings

"Oh dear, I *am* disappointed. I was hoping it might be a ticket for the Irish Sweep."

"There's no reason to be disappointed," Cyril Bixby said. "As a matter of fact this could be rather amusing."

"Why could it be amusing, darling?"

He began explaining to her exactly how a pawn ticket worked, with particular reference to the fact that anyone possessing the ticket was entitled to claim the article. She listened patiently until he had finished his lecture.

"You think it's worth claiming?" she asked.

"I think it's worth finding out what it is. You see this figure of fifty dollars that's written here? You know what that means?"

"No, dear, what does it mean?"

"It means that the item in question is almost certain to be something quite valuable."

"You mean it'll be worth fifty dollars?"

"More like five hundred."

"Five hundred!"

"Don't you understand?" he said. "A pawnbroker never gives you more than about a tenth of the real value."

"Good gracious! I never knew that."

"There's a lot of things you don't know, my dear. Now you listen to me. Seeing that there's no name and address of the owner . . ."

"But surely there's something to say who it belongs to?"

"Not a thing. People often do that. They don't want anyone to know they've been to a pawnbroker. They're ashamed of it."

"Then you think we can keep it?"

"Of course we can keep it. This is now *our* ticket."

"You mean *my* ticket," Mrs Bixby said firmly. "I found it."

"My dear girl, what *does* it matter? The important thing is that we are now in a position to go and redeem it any time we like for only fifty dollars. How about that?"

"Oh, what fun!" she cried. "I think it's terribly exciting, especially when we don't even know what it is. It could be *anything*, isn't that right, Cyril? Absolutely anything!"

"It could indeed, although it's most likely to be either a ring or a watch."

"But wouldn't it be marvellous if it was a *real* treasure? I mean something *really* old, like a wonderful old vase or a Roman statue."

"There's no knowing what it might be, my dear. We shall

just have to wait and see."

"I think it's absolutely fascinating! Give me the ticket and I'll rush over first thing Monday morning and find out!"

"I think I'd better do that."

"Oh no!" she cried. "Let *me* do it!"

"I think not. I'll pick it up on my way to work."

"But it's *my* ticket! *Please* let me do it, Cyril! Why should *you* have all the fun?"

"You don't know these pawnbrokers, my dear. You're liable to get cheated."

"I wouldn't get cheated, honestly I wouldn't. Give it to me, please."

"Also you have to have fifty dollars," he said, smiling. "You have to pay out fifty dollars in cash before they'll give it to you."

"I've got that," she said. "I think."

"I'd rather you didn't handle it, if you don't mind."

"But Cyril, *I found* it. It's mine. Whatever it is, it's mine, isn't that right?"

"Of course it's yours, my dear. There's no need to get so worked up about it."

"I'm not. I'm just excited, that's all."

"I suppose it hasn't occurred to you that this might be something entirely masculine – a pocket-watch, for example, or a set of shirt-studs. It isn't only women that go to pawnbrokers, you know."

"In that case I'll give it to you for Christmas," Mrs Bixby said magnanimously.[1] "I'll be delighted. But if it's a woman's thing, I want it myself. Is that agreed?"

"That sounds very fair. Why don't you come with me when I collect it?"

Mrs Bixby was about to say yes to this, but caught herself just in time. She had no wish to be greeted like an old customer by the pawnbroker in her husband's presence.

"No," she said slowly. "I don't think I will. You see, it'll be even more thrilling if I stay behind and wait. Oh, I do hope it isn't going to be something that neither of us wants."

"You've got a point there," he said. "If I don't think it's worth fifty dollars, I won't even take it."

"But you said it would be worth five hundred."

"I'm quite sure it will. Don't worry."

[1] generously

"Oh, Cyril, I can hardly wait! Isn't it exciting?"

"It's amusing," he said, slipping the ticket into his waistcoat pocket. "There's no doubt about that."

Monday morning came at last, and after breakfast Mrs Bixby followed her husband to the door and helped him on with his coat.

"Don't work too hard, darling," she said.

"No, all right."

"Home at six?"

"I hope so."

"Are you going to have time to go to that pawnbroker?" she asked.

"My God, I forgot all about it. I'll take a cab and go there now. It's on my way."

"You haven't lost the ticket, have you?"

"I hope not," he said, feeling in his waistcoat pocket. "No, here it is."

"And you have enough money?"

"Just about."

"Darling," she said, standing close to him and straightening his tie, which was perfectly straight. "If it happens to be something nice, something you think I might like, will you telephone me as soon as you get to the office?"

"If you want me to, yes."

"You know, I'm sort of hoping it'll be something for you, Cyril. I'd much rather it was for you than for me."

"That's very generous of you, my dear. Now I must run."

About an hour later, when the telephone rang, Mrs Bixby was across the room so fast she had the receiver off the hook before the first ring had finished.

"I got it!" he said.

"You did! Oh, Cyril, what was it? Was it something good?"

"Good!" he cried. "It's fantastic! You wait till you get your eyes on this! You'll swoon!"

"Darling, what is it? Tell me quick!"

"You're a lucky girl, that's what you are."

"It's for me, then?"

"Of course it's for you. Though how in the world it ever got to be pawned for only fifty dollars I'll be damned if I know. Someone's crazy."

"Cyril! Stop keeping me in suspense! I can't bear it!"

"You'll go mad when you see it."

"What is it?"

"Try to guess."

Mrs Bixby paused. Be careful, she told herself. Be very careful now.

"A necklace," she said.

"Wrong."

"A diamond ring."

"You're not even warm. I'll give you a hint. It's something you can wear."

"Something I can wear? You mean like a hat?"

"No, it's not a hat," he said, laughing.

"For goodness sake, Cyril! Why don't you tell me?"

"Because I want it to be a surprise. I'll bring it home with me this evening."

"You'll do nothing of the sort!" she cried. "I'm coming right down there to get it now!"

"I'd rather you didn't do that."

"Don't be so silly, darling. Why shouldn't I come?"

"Because I'm too busy. You'll disorganize my whole morning schedule. I'm half an hour behind already."

"Then I'll come in the lunch hour. All right?"

"I'm not having a lunch hour. Oh well, come at one-thirty then, while I'm having a sandwich. Good-bye."

At half past one precisely, Mrs Bixby arrived at Mr Bixby's place of business and rang the bell. Her husband, in his white dentist's coat, opened the door himself.

"Oh, Cyril, I'm so excited!"

"So you should be. You're a lucky girl, did you know that?" He led her down the passage and into the surgery.

"Go and have your lunch, Miss Pulteney," he said to the assistant, who was busy putting instruments into the sterilizer. "You can finish that when you come back." He waited until the girl had gone, then he walked over to a closet that he used for hanging up his clothes and stood in front of it, pointing with his finger. "It's in there," he said. "Now – shut your eyes."

Mrs Bixby did as she was told. Then she took a deep breath and held it, and in the silence that followed she could hear him opening the cupboard door and there was a soft swishing sound as he pulled out a garment from among the other things hanging there.

"All right! You can look!"

"I don't dare to," she said, laughing.

"Go on. Take a peek."

Coyly, beginning to giggle, she raised one eyelid a fraction of an inch, just enough to give her a dark blurry view of the man standing there in his white overalls holding something up in the air.

"Mink!" he cried. "Real mink!"

At the sound of the magic word she opened her eyes quick, and at the same time she actually started forward in order to clasp the coat in her arms.

But there was no coat. There was only a ridiculous little fur neckpiece dangling from her husband's hand.

"Feast your eyes on that!" he said, waving it in front of her face.

Mrs Bixby put a hand up to her mouth and started backing away. I'm going to scream, she told herself. I just know it. I'm going to scream.

"What's the matter, my dear? Don't you like it?" He stopped waving the fur and stood staring at her, waiting for her to say something.

"Why yes," she stammered. "I . . . I . . . think it's . . . it's lovely . . . really lovely."

"Quite took your breath away for a moment there, didn't it?"

"Yes, it did."

"Magnificent quality," he said. "Fine colour, too. You know something, my dear? I reckon a piece like this would cost you two or three hundred dollars at least if you had to buy it in a shop."

"I don't doubt it."

There were two skins, two narrow mangy-looking skins with their heads still on them and glass beads in their eye sockets and little paws hanging down. One of them had the rear end of the other in its mouth, biting it.

"Here," he said. "Try it on." He leaned forward and draped the thing around her neck, then stepped back to admire. "It's perfect. It really suits you. It isn't everyone who has mink, my dear."

"No, it isn't."

"Better leave it behind when you go shopping or they'll all think we're millionaires and start charging us double."

"I'll try to remember that, Cyril."

"I'm afraid you mustn't expect anything else for Christmas. Fifty dollars was rather more than I was going to spend anyway."

He turned away and went over to the basin and began washing his hands. "Run along now, my dear, and buy yourself a nice lunch. I'd take you out myself but I've got old man Gorman in the waiting-room with a broken clasp on his denture."

Mrs Bixby moved towards the door.

I'm going to kill that pawnbroker, she told herself. I'm going right back there to the shop this very minute and I'm going to throw this filthy neckpiece right in his face and if he refuses to give me back my coat I'm going to kill him.

"Did I tell you I was going to be late home tonight?" Cyril Bixby said, still washing his hands.

"No."

"It'll probably be at least eight-thirty the way things look at the moment. It may even be nine."

"Yes, all right. Good-bye." Mrs Bixby went out, slamming the door behind her.

At that precise moment, Miss Pulteney, the secretary-assistant, came sailing past her down the corridor on her way to lunch.

"Isn't it a gorgeous day?" Miss Pulteney said as she went by, flashing a smile. There was lilt in her walk, a little whiff of perfume attending her, and she looked like a queen, just exactly like a queen in the beautiful black mink coat that the Colonel had given to Mrs Bixby.

ForeSkin

Skin

That year – 1946 – winter was a long time going. Although it was April, a freezing wind blew through the streets of the city, and overhead the snow clouds moved across the sky.

The old man who was called Drioli shuffled painfully along the sidewalk of the rue de Rivoli. He was cold and miserable, huddled up like a hedgehog in a filthy black coat, only his eyes and the top of his head visible above the turned-up collar.

The door of a café opened and the faint whiff of roasting chicken brought a pain of yearning to the top of his stomach. He moved on glancing without any interest at the things in the shop windows – perfume, silk ties and shirts, diamonds, porcelain, antique furniture, finely bound books. Then a picture gallery. He had always liked picture galleries. This one had a single canvas on display in the window. He stopped to look at it. He turned to go on. He checked, looked back; and now, suddenly, there came to him a slight uneasiness, a movement of the memory, a distant recollection of something, somewhere, he had seen before. He looked again. It was a landscape, a clump of trees leaning madly over to one side as if blown by a tremendous wind, the sky swirling and twisting all around. Attached to the frame there was a little plaque, and on this it said: CHAIM SOUTINE[1] (1894–1943).

Drioli stared at the picture, wondering vaguely what there was about it that seemed familiar. Crazy painting, he thought. Very strange and crazy – but I like it ... Chaim Soutine ... Soutine ... "By God!" he cried suddenly. "My little Kalmuck,[2] that's who it is! My little Kalmuck with a picture in the finest shop in Paris! Just imagine that!"

The old man pressed his face closer to the window. He could remember the boy – yes, quite clearly he could remember him. But when? The rest of it was not so easy to recollect. It was

[1] a Russian painter, who lived most of his life as a recluse in Paris
[2] a person from Mongolia – here a nickname

so long ago. How long? Twenty – no, more like thirty years, wasn't it? Wait a minute. Yes – it was the year before the war, the first war, 1913. That was it. And this Soutine, this ugly little Kalmuck, a sullen brooding boy whom he had liked – almost loved – for no reason at all that he could think of except that he could paint.

And how he could paint! It was coming back more clearly now – the street, the line of refuse cans along the length of it, the rotten smell, the brown cats walking delicately over the refuse, and then the women, moist fat women sitting on the doorsteps with their feet upon the cobblestones of the street. Which street? Where was it the boy had lived?

The Cité Falguière, that was it! The old man nodded his head several times, pleased to have remembered the name. Then there was the studio with the single chair in it, and the filthy red couch that the boy had used for sleeping; the drunken parties, the cheap white wine, the furious quarrels, and always, always the bitter sullen face of the boy brooding over his work.

It was odd, Drioli thought, how easily it all came back to him now, how each single small remembered fact seemed instantly to remind him of another.

There was that nonsense with the tattoo, for instance. Now, *that* was a mad thing if ever there was one. How had it started? Ah, yes – he had got rich one day, that was it, and he had bought lots of wine. He could see himself now as he entered the studio with the parcel of bottles under his arm – the boy sitting before the easel, and his (Drioli's) own wife standing in the centre of the room, posing for her picture.

"Tonight we shall celebrate," he said. "We shall have a little celebration, us three."

"What is it that we celebrate?" the boy asked, without looking up. "Is it that you have decided to divorce your wife so she can marry me?"

"No," Drioli said. "We celebrate because today I have made a great sum of money with my work."

"And I have made nothing. We can celebrate that also."

"If you like." Drioli was standing by the table unwrapping the parcel. He felt tired and he wanted to get at the wine. Nine clients in one day was all very nice, but it could play hell with a man's eyes. He had never done as many as nine before. Nine boozy soldiers – and the remarkable thing was that no fewer than seven of them had been able to pay in cash. This had made him extremely rich. But the work was terrible on the eyes. Drioli's eyes were half closed from fatigue, the whites streaked with little connecting lines of red; and about an inch behind each eyeball there was a small concentration of pain. But it was evening now and he was wealthy as a pig, and in the parcel there were three bottles – one for his wife, one for his friend, and one for him. He had found the corkscrew and was drawing the corks from the bottles, each making a small plop as it came out.

The boy put down his brush. "Oh, Christ," he said. "How can one work with all this going on?"

The girl came across the room to look at the painting. Drioli came over also, holding a bottle in one hand, a glass in the other.

"No!" the boy shouted, blazing up suddenly. "Please – no!" He snatched the canvas from the easel and stood it against the wall. But Drioli had seen it.

"I like it."

"It's terrible."

"It's marvellous. Like all the others that you do, it's marvellous. I love them all."

"The trouble is," the boy said, scowling, "that in themselves they are not nourishing. I cannot eat them."

"But still they are marvellous." Drioli handed him a tumblerful of the pale-yellow wine. "Drink it," he said. "It will make you happy."

Never, he thought, had he known a more unhappy person, or one with a gloomier face. He had spotted him in a café some seven months before, drinking alone, and because he had looked like a Russian or some sort of an Asiatic, Drioli had sat down at his table and talked.

"You are a Russian?"

"Yes."

"Where from?"

"Minsk."

Drioli had jumped up and embraced him, crying that he too had been born in that city.

"It wasn't actually Minsk," the boy had said. "But quite near."

"Where?"

"Smilovichi, about twelve miles away."

"Smilovichi!" Drioli had shouted, embracing him again. "I walked there several times when I was a boy." Then he had sat down again, staring affectionately at the other's face. "You know," he had said, "you don't look like a western Russian. You're like a Tartar, or a Kalmuck. You look exactly like a Kalmuck."

Now, standing in the studio, Drioli looked again at the boy as he took the glass of wine and tipped it down his throat in one swallow. Yes, he did have a face like a Kalmuck – very broad and high-cheeked, with a wide coarse nose. This broadness of the cheeks was accentuated by the ears which stood out sharply from the head. And then he had the narrow eyes, the black hair, the thick sullen mouth of a Kalmuck, but the hands – the hands were always a surprise, so small and white like a lady's, with tiny thin fingers.

"Give me some more," the boy said. "If we are to celebrate then let us do it properly."

Drioli distributed the wine and sat himself on a chair. The boy sat on the old couch with Drioli's wife. The three bottles were placed on the floor between them.

"Tonight we shall drink as much as we possibly can," Drioli said. "I am exceptionally rich. I think perhaps I should go out now and buy some more bottles. How many shall I get?"

"Six more," the boy said. "Two for each."

"Good. I shall go now and fetch them."

"And I will help you."

In the nearest café Drioli bought six bottles of white wine, and they carried them back to the studio. They placed them on the floor in two rows, and Drioli fetched the corkscrew and pulled the corks, all six of them; then they sat down again and continued to drink.

"It is only the very wealthy," Drioli said, "who can afford to celebrate in this manner."

"That is true," the boy said. "Isn't that true, Josie?"

"Of course."

"How do you feel, Josie?"

"Fine."

"Will you leave Drioli and marry me?"

"No."

"Beautiful wine," Drioli said. "It is a privilege to drink it."

Slowly, methodically, they set about getting themselves drunk. The process was routine, but all the same there was a certain ceremony to be observed, and a gravity to be maintained, and a great number of things to be said, then said again – and the wine must be praised, and the slowness was important too, so that there would be time to savour the three delicious stages of transition, especially (for Drioli) the one when he began to float and his feet did not really belong to him. That was the best period of them all – when he could look down at his feet and they were so far away that he would wonder what crazy person they might belong to and why they were lying around on the floor like that, in the distance.

After a while, he got up to switch on the light. He was surprised to see that the feet came with him when he did this, especially because he couldn't feel them touching the ground. It gave him a pleasant sensation of walking on air. Then he began wandering around the room, peeking slyly at the canvases stacked against the walls.

"Listen," he said at length. "I have an idea." He came across and stood before the couch, swaying gently. "Listen, my little Kalmuck."

"What?"

"I have a tremendous idea. Are you listening?"

"I'm listening to Josie."

"Listen to me, *please*. You are my friend – my ugly little Kalmuck from Minsk – and to me you are such an artist that I would like to have a picture, a lovely picture – "

"Have them all. Take all you can find, but do not interrupt me when I am talking with your wife."

"No, no. Now listen. I mean a picture that I can have with me always . . . for ever . . . wherever I go . . . whatever happens . . . but always with me . . . a picture by you." He reached forward and shook the boy's knee. "Now listen to me, *please*."

"Listen to him," the girl said.

"It is this. I want you to paint a picture on my skin, on my back. Then I want you to tattoo over what you have painted so that it will be there always."

"You have crazy ideas."

"I will teach you how to use the tattoo. It is easy. A child could do it."

"I am not a child."

"*Please* . . ."

"You are quite mad. What is it you want?" The painter looked up into the slow, dark, wine-bright eyes of the other man. What in heaven's name is it you want?"

"You could do it easily! You could! You could!"

"You mean with the tattoo?"

"Yes, with the tattoo! I will teach you in two minutes!"

"Impossible!"

"Are you saying I do not know what I am talking about?"

No, the boy could not possibly be saying that because if anyone knew about the tattoo it was he – Drioli. Had he not, only last month, covered a man's whole belly with the most wonderful and delicate design composed entirely of flowers? What about the client who had had so much hair upon his chest that he had done him a picture of a grizzly bear so designed that the hair on the chest became the furry coat of the bear? Could he not draw the likeness of a lady and position it with such subtlety upon a man's arm that when the muscle of the arm was flexed the lady came to life and performed some astonishing contortions?

"All I am saying," the boy told him, "is that you are drunk and this is a drunken idea."

"We could have Josie for a model. A study of Josie upon my back. Am I not entitled to a picture of my wife upon my back?"

"Of Josie?"

"Yes." Drioli knew he only had to mention his wife and the boy's thick brown lips would loosen and begin to quiver.

"No," the girl said.

"Darling Josie, *please*. Take this bottle and finish it, then you will feel more generous. It is an enormous idea. Never in my life have I had such an idea before."

"What idea?"

"That he should make a picture of you upon my back. Am I not entitled to that?"

"A picture of me?"

"A nude study," the boy said. "It is an agreeable idea."

"Not nude," the girl said.

"It is an enormous idea," Drioli said.

"It's a damn crazy idea," the girl said.

"It is in any event an idea," the boy said. "It is an idea that calls for a celebration."

They emptied another bottle among them. Then the boy said, "It is no good. I could not possibly manage the tattoo. Instead, I will paint this picture on your back and you will have it with you so long as you do not take a bath and wash it off. If you never take a bath again in your life then you will have it always, as long as you live."

"No," Drioli said.

"Yes – and on the day that you decide to take a bath I will know that you do not any longer value my picture. It will be a test of your admiration for my art."

"I do not like the idea," the girl said. "His admiration for your art is so great that he would be unclean for many years. Let us have the tattoo. But not nude."

"Then just the head," Drioli said.

"I could not manage it."

"It is immensely simple. I will undertake to teach you in two minutes. You will see. I shall go now and fetch the instruments. The needles and the inks. I have inks of many different colours – as many different colours as you have paints, and far more beautiful . . . "

"It is impossible."

"I have many inks. Have I not many different colours of inks, Josie?"

"Yes."

"You will see," Drioli said. "I will go now and fetch them." He got up from his chair and walked unsteadily, but with determination, out of the room.

In half an hour Drioli was back. "I have brought everything," he cried, waving a brown suitcase. "All the necessities of the tattooist are here in this bag."

He placed the bag on the table, opened it, and laid out the electric needles and the small bottles of coloured inks. He plugged in the electric needle, then he took the instrument in his hand and pressed a switch. It made a buzzing sound and the quarter inch of needle that projected from the end of it began to vibrate swiftly up and down. He threw off his jacket and rolled up his left sleeve. "Now look. Watch me and I will show you how easy it is. I will make a design on my arm, here."

His forearm was already covered with blue markings, but he selected a small clear patch of skin upon which to demonstrate.

"First, I choose my ink – let us use ordinary blue – and I dip the point of the needle in the ink . . . so . . . and I hold the needle up straight and I run it lightly over the surface of the skin . . . like this . . . and with the little motor and the electricity, the needle jumps up and down and punctures the skin and the ink goes in and there you are. See how easy it is . . . see how I draw a picture of a greyhound here upon my arm . . . "

The boy was intrigued. "Now let *me* practise a little – on your arm."

With the buzzing needle he began to draw blue lines upon Drioli's arm. "It is simple," he said. "It is like drawing with pen and ink. There is no difference except that it is slower."

"There is nothing to it. Are you ready? Shall we begin?"

"At once."

"There model!" cried Drioll. "Come on, Josie!" He was in a bustle of enthusiasm now, tottering around the room arranging everything, like a child preparing for some exciting game, "Where will you have her? Where shall she stand?"

"Let her be standing there, by my dressing-table. Let her be brushing her hair. I will paint her with her hair down over her shoulders and her brushing it."

"Tremendous. You are a genius."

Reluctantly, the girl walked over and stood by the dressing table, carrying her glass of wine with her.

Drioli pulled off his shirt and stepped out of his trousers. He retained only his underpants and his socks and shoes, and he stood there swaying gently from side to side, his small body firm, white-skinned, almost hairless. "Now," he said, "I am the canvas. Where will you place your canvas?"

"As always, upon the easel."

"Don't be crazy. I am the canvas."

"Then place yourself upon the easel. That is where you belong."

"How can I?"

"Are you the canvas or are you not the canvas?"

"I am the canvas. Already I begin to feel like a canvas."

"Then place yourself upon the easel. There should be no difficulty."

"Truly, it is not possible."

"Then sit on the chair. Sit back to front, then you can lean your drunken head against the back of it. Hurry now, for I am about to commence."

"I am ready. I am waiting."

"First," the boy said, "I shall make an ordinary painting. Then, if it pleases me, I shall tattoo over it." With a wide brush he began to paint upon the naked skin of the man's back.

"Ayee! Ayee!" Drioli screamed. "A monstrous centipede is marching down my spine!"

"Be still now! Be still" The boy worked rapidly, applying the paint only in a thin blue wash so that it would not afterwards interfere with the process of tattooing. His concentration, as soon as he began to paint, was so great that it appeared some-how to supersede his drunkenness. He applied the brush strokes with quick short jabs of the arm, holding the wrist stiff, and in less than half an hour it was finished.

"All right. That's all," he said to the girl, who immediately returned to the couch, lay down, and fell asleep.

Drioli remained awake. He watched the boy take up the needle and dip it in the ink; then he felt the sharp ticking sting as it touched the skin of his back. The pain, which was un-pleasant but never extreme, kept him from going to sleep. By following the track of the needle and by watching the different colours of ink that the boy was using, Drioli amused himself trying to visualize what was going on behind him. The boy worked with an astonishing intensity. He appeared to have become completely absorbed in the little machine and in the unusual effects it was able to produce.

Far into the small hours of the morning the machine buzzed and the boy worked. Drioli could remember that when the artist finally stepped back and said, "It is finished," there was daylight outside and the sound of people walking in the street.

"I want to see it," Drioli said. The boy held up a mirror, at an angle, and Drioli craned his neck to look.

"Good God!" he cried. It was a startling sight. The whole of his back, from the top of the shoulders to the base of the spine, was a blaze of colour – gold and green and blue and black and scarlet. The tattoo was applied so heavily it looked almost like an impasto.[1] The boy had followed as closely as possible the original brush strokes, filling them in solid, and it was marvellous the way he had made use of the spine and the pro-trusion of the shoulder blades so that they became part of the composition. What is more, he had somehow managed to achieve – even with this slow process – a certain spontaneity. The portrait was quite alive; it contained much of that twisted, tortured quality so characteristic of Soutine's other work. It was not a good likeness. It was a mood rather than likeness, the model's face vague and tipsy, the background swirling around her head in a mass of dark-green curling strokes.

"It's tremendous!"

[1] a painting with many thick, paste-like layers

"I rather like it myself." They boy stood back, examining it critically. "You know," he added, "I think it's good enough for me to sign." And taking up the buzzer again, he inscribed his name in red ink on the right-hand side, over the place where Drioli's kidney was.

The old man who was called Drioli was standing in a sort of trance, staring at the painting in the window of the picture-dealer's shop. It had been so long ago, all that – almost as though it had happened in another life.

And the boy? What had become of him? He could remember now that after returning from the war – the first war – he had missed him and had questioned Josie.

"Where is my little Kalmuck?"

"He is gone," she had answered. "I do not know where, but I heard it said that a dealer had taken him up and sent him away to Céret to make more paintings."

"Perhaps he will return."

"Perhaps he will. Who knows?"

That was the last time they had mentioned him. Shortly afterwards they had moved to Le Havre[1] where there were more sailors and business was better. The old man smiled as he remembered Le Havre. Those were the pleasant years, the years between the wars, with the small shop near the docks and the comfortable rooms and always enough work, with every day three, four, five sailors coming and wanting pictures on their arms. Those were truly the pleasant years.

Then had come the second war, and Josie being killed, and the Germans arriving, and that was the finish of his business. No one had wanted pictures on their arms any more after that. And by that time he was too old for any other kind of work. In desperation he had made his way back to Paris, hoping vaguely that things would be easier in the big city. But they were not.

And now, after the war was over, he possessed neither the means nor the energy to start up his small business again. It wasn't very easy for an old man to know what to do, especially when one did not like to beg. Yet how else could he keep alive?

Well, he thought, still staring at the picture. So that is my little Kalmuck. And how quickly the sight of one small object such as this can stir the memory. Up to a few moments ago he

[1] French channel port

had even forgotten that he had a tattoo on his back. It had been ages since he had thought about it. He put his face closer to the window and looked into the gallery. On the walls he could see many other pictures and all seemed to be the work of the same artist. There were a great number of people strolling around. Obviously it was a special exhibition.

On a sudden impulse, Drioli turned, pushed open the door of the gallery and went in.

It was a long room with a thick wine-coloured carpet, and by God how beautiful and warm it was! There were all these people strolling about looking at the pictures, well-washed dignified people, each of whom held a catalogue in the hand. Drioli stood just inside the door, nervously glancing around, wondering whether he dared go forward and mingle with this crowd. But before he had had time to gather his courage, he heard a voice beside him saying. "What is it you want?"

The speaker wore a black morning coat. He was plump and short and had a very white face. It was a flabby face with so much flesh upon it that the cheeks hung down on either side of the mouth in two fleshy collops,[1] spanielwise. He came up close to Drioli and said again, "What is it you want?"

Drioli stood still.

"If you please," the man was saying, "take yourself out of my gallery."

"Am I not permitted to look at the pictures?"

"I have asked you to leave."

Drioli stood his ground. He felt suddenly, overwhelmingly outraged.

"Let us not have trouble," the man was saying. "Come on now, this way." He put a fat white paw on Drioli's arm and began to push him firmly to the door.

That did it. "Take your goddam hands off me!" Drioli shouted. His voice rang clear down the long gallery and all the heads jerked around as one – all the startled faces stared down the length of the room at the person who had made this noise. A flunkey[2] came running over to help, and the two men tried to hustle Drioli through the door. The people stood still, watching the struggle. Their faces expressed only a mild interest, and seemed to be saying. "It's all right. There's no danger to us.

---

[1] slices of meat
[2] assistant

It's being taken care of."

"I, too!" Drioli was shouting. "I too, have a picture by this painter! He was my friend and I have a picture which he gave me!"

"He's mad."

"A lunatic. A raving lunatic."

"Someone should call the police."

With a rapid twist of the body Drioli suddenly jumped clear of the two men, and before anyone could stop him he was running down the gallery shouting. "I'll show you! I'll show you! I'll show you!" He flung off his overcoat, then his jacket and shirt, and he turned so that his naked back was towards the people.

"There!" he cried, breathing quickly. "You see? There it is!"

There was a sudden absolute silence in the room, each person arrested in what he was doing, standing motionless in a kind of shocked, uneasy bewilderment. They were staring at the tattooed picture. It was still there, the colours as bright as ever, but the old man's back was thinner now, the shoulder blades protruded more sharply, and the effect, though not great, was to give the picture a curiously wrinkled, squashed appearance.

Somebody said, "My God, but it is!"

Then came the excitement and the noise of voices as the people surged forward to crowd around the old man.

"It is unmistakable!"

"His early manner, yes?"

"It is fantastic, fantastic!"

"And look, it is signed!"

"Bend your shoulders forward, my friend, so that the picture stretches out flat."

"Old one, when was this done?"

"In 1913," Drioli said, without turning around. "In the autumn of 1913."

"Who taught Soutine to tattoo?"

"I taught him."

"And the woman?"

"She was my wife."

The gallery owner was pushing through the crowd towards Drioli. He was calm now, deadly serious, making a smile with his mouth. "Monsieur," he said. "I will buy it." Drioli could see the loose fat upon the face vibrating as he moved his jaw. "I said I will buy it, Monsieur."

"How can you buy it?" Drioli asked softly.

"I will give two hundred thousand francs for it." The dealer's eyes were small and dark, the wings of his broad nose-base were beginning to quiver.

"Don't do it!" someone murmured in the crowd. "It is worth twenty times as much."

Drioli opened his mouth to speak. No words came, so he shut it; then he opened it again and said slowly. "But how can I sell it?" He lifted his hands, let them drop loosely to his sides. "Monsieur, how can I possibly sell it!" All the sadness in the world was in his voice.

"Yes!" they were saying in the crowd. "How can he sell it? It is part of himself!"

"Listen," the dealer said, coming up close. "I will help you. I will make you rich. Together we shall make some private arrangement over this picture, no?"

Drioli watched him with slow, apprehensive eyes. "But how can you buy it, Monsieur? What will you do with it when you have bought it? Where will you keep it? Where will you keep it tonight? And where tomorrow?"

"Ah, where will I keep it? Yes, where will I keep it? Now, where will I keep it? Well, now ... " The dealer stroked the bridge of his nose with a fat white finger. "It would seem," he said, "that if I take the picture, I take you also. That is a disadvantage." He paused and stroked his nose again. "The picture itself is of no value until you are dead. How old are you, my friend?"

"Sixty-one."

"But you are perhaps not very robust, no?" The dealer lowered the hand from his nose and looked Drioli up and down, slowly, like a farmer appraising an old horse.

"I do not like this," Drioli said, edging away. "Quite honestly, Monsieur, I do not like it." He edged straight into the arms of a tall man who put out his hands and caught him gently by the shoulders. Drioli glanced around and apologized. The man smiled down at him, patting one of the old fellow's naked shoulders reassuringly with a hand encased in a canary-coloured glove.

"Listen, my friend," the stranger said, still smiling. "Do you like to swim and to bask yourself in the sun?"

Drioli looked up at him, rather startled.

"Do you like fine food and red wine from the great châteaux

of Bordeaux?" The man was still smiling, showing strong white teeth with a flash of gold among them. He spoke in a soft coaxing manner, one gloved hand still resting on Drioli's shoulder. "Do you like such things?"

"Well – yes," Drioli answered, still greatly perplexed. "Of course."

"And the company of beautiful women?"

"Why not?"

"And a cupboard full of suits and shirts made to your own personal measurements? It would seem that you are a little lacking for clothes."

Drioli watched this suave man, waiting for the rest of the proposition.

"Have you ever had a shoe constructed especially for your own foot?"

"No."

"You would like that?"

"Well ... "

"And a man who will shave you in the mornings and trim your hair?"

Drioli simply stood and gaped.

"And a plump attractive girl to manicure the nails of your fingers?"

Someone in the crowd giggled.

"And a bell beside your bed to summon a maid to bring your breakfast in the morning? Would you like these things, my friend? Do they appeal to you?"

Drioli stood still and looked at him.

"You see, I am the owner of the Hotel Bristol in Cannes. I now invite you to come down there and live as my guest for the rest of your life in luxury and comfort." The man paused, allowing his listener time to savour this cheerful prospect.

"Your only duty – shall I call it your pleasure – will be to spend your time on my beach in bathing trunks, walking among my guests, sunning yourself, swimming, drinking cocktails. You would like that?"

There was no answer.

"Don't you see – all the guests will thus be able to observe this fascinating picture by Soutine. You will become famous, and men will say, 'Look, there is the fellow with ten million francs upon his back.' You like this idea, Monsieur? It pleases you?"

Drioli looked up at the tall man in the canary gloves, still wondering whether this was some sort of a joke. "It is a comical idea," he said slowly. "But do you really mean it?"

"Of course I mean it."

"Wait," the dealer interrupted. "See here, old one. Here is the answer to our problem. I will buy the picture, and I will arrange with a surgeon to remove the skin from your back, and then you will be able to go off on your own and enjoy the great sum of money I shall give you for it."

"With no skin on my back?"

"No, no, please! You misunderstand. This surgeon will put a new piece of skin in the place of the old one. It is simple."

"Could he do that?"

"There is nothing to it."

"Impossible!" said the man with the canary gloves. "He's too old for such a major skin-grafting operation. It would kill him. It would kill you, my friend."

"It would kill me?"

"Naturally. You would never survive. Only the picture would come through."

"In the name of God!" Drioli cried. He looked around aghast at the faces of the people watching him, and in the silence that followed, another man's voice, speaking quietly from the back of the group, could be heard saying, "Perhaps, if one were to offer this old man enough money, he might consent to kill himself on the spot. Who knows?" A few people sniggered. The dealer moved his feet uneasily on the carpet.

Then the hand in the canary glove was tapping Drioli again upon the shoulder. "Come on," the man was saying, smiling his broad white smile. "You and I will go and have a good dinner and we can talk about it some more while we eat. How's that? Are you hungry?"

Drioli watched him, frowning. He didn't like the man's long flexible neck, or the way he craned it forward at you when he spoke, like a snake.

"Roast duck and Chambertin,"[1] the man was saying. He put a rich succulent accent on the words, splashing them out with his tongue. "And perhaps a soufflé aux marrons, light and frothy."

Drioli's eyes turned up towards the ceiling, his lips became

---

[1] a famous French red wine

loose and wet. One could see the poor old fellow beginning literally to drool at the mouth.

"How do you like your duck?" the man went on. "Do you like it very brown and crisp outside, or shall it be . . ."

"I am coming," Drioli said quickly. Already he had picked up his shirt and was pulling it frantically over his head. "Wait for me, Monsieur. I am coming." And within a minute he had disappeared out of the gallery with his new patron.

It wasn't more than a few weeks later that a picture by Soutine, of a woman's head, painted in an unusual manner, nicely framed and heavily varnished, turned up for sale in Buenos Aires. That – and the fact that there is no hotel in Cannes called Bristol – causes one to wonder a little, and to pray for the old man's health, and to hope fervently that wherever he may be at this moment, there is a plump attractive girl to manicure the nails of his fingers, and a maid to bring him his breakfast in bed in the morning.

The Ratcatcher

The Ratcatcher

In the afternoon the ratcatcher came to the filling station. He came sidling up the driveway with a stealthy, soft-treading gait, making no noise at all with his feet on the gravel. He had an army knapsack slung over one shoulder and he was wearing an old-fashioned black jacket with large pockets. His brown corduroy trousers were tied around the knees with pieces of white string.

"Yes?" Claud asked, knowing very well who he was.

"Rodent operative." His small dark eyes moved swiftly over the premises.

"The ratcatcher?"

"That's me."

The man was lean and brown with a sharp face and two long sulphur-coloured teeth that protruded from the upper jaw, overlapping the lower lip, pressing it inward. The ears were thin and pointed and set far back on the head, near the nape of the neck. The eyes were almost black, but when they looked at you there was a flash of yellow somewhere inside them.

"You've come very quick."

"Special orders from the Health Officer."

"And now you're going to catch all the rats?"

"Yep."

The kind of dark furtive eyes he had were those of an animal that lives its life peering out cautiously and forever from a hole in the ground.

"How are you going to catch 'em?"

"Ah-h-h," the ratman said darkly. "That's all accordin' to where they is."

"Trap 'em, I suppose."

"Trap 'em!" he cried, disgusted. "You won't catch many rats that way! Rats isn't rabbits, you know."

He held his face up high, sniffing the air with a nose, that twitched perceptibly from side to side.

"No," he said, scornfully. "Trappin's no way to catch a rat.

Rats is clever, let me tell you that. If you want to catch 'em, you got to know 'em. You got to know rats on this job."

I could see Claud staring at him with a certain fascination.

"They're more clever'n dogs, rats is."

"Get away."

"You know what they do? They watch you! All the time you're goin' round preparin' to catch 'em, they're sittin' quietly in dark places, watchin' you.' The man crouched, stretching his stringy neck far forward.

"So what do you do?" Claud asked, fascinated.

"Ah! That's it, you see. That's where you got to know rats."

"How d'you catch 'em?"

"There's ways," the ratman said, leering. "There's various ways."

He paused, nodding his repulsive head sagely up and down. "It's all dependin'," he said, "on where they is. This ain't a sewer job, is it?"

"No, it's not a sewer job."

"Tricky things, sewer jobs. Yes," he said, delicately sniffing the air to the left of him with his mobile nose-end, "sewer jobs is very tricky things."

"Not especially, I shouldn't think."

"Oh-ho. You shouldn't, shouldn't you! Well, I'd like to see *you* do a sewer job! Just exactly how would *you* set about it, I'd like to know?"

"Nothing to it. I'd just poison 'em, that's all."

"And where exactly would you put the poison, might I ask?"

"Down the sewer. Where the hell you think I put it!"

"There!" the ratman cried, triumphant. "I knew it! Down the sewer! And you know what'd happen then? Get washed away, that's all. Sewer's like a river, y'know."

"That's what *you* say," Claud answered. "That's only what *you* say."

"It's facts."

"All right, then, all right. So what would *you* do, Mr Know-all?"

"That's exactly where you got to know rats, on a sewer job."

"Come on then, let's have it."

"Now listen. I'll tell you." The ratman advanced a step closer, his voice became secretive and confidential, the voice of a man divulging fabulous professional secrets. "You works on the understandin' that a rat is a gnawin' animal, see. Rats *gnaws*.

Anythin' you give 'em, don't matter what it is, anything new they never seen before, and what do they do? They *gnaws* it. So now! There are you! You get a sewer job on your hands. And what d'you do?"

His voice had the soft throaty sound of a croaking frog and he seemed to speak all his words with an immense wet-lipped relish, as though they tasted good on the tongue. The accent was similar to Claud's, the broad soft accent of the Buckinghamshire countryside, but his voice was more throaty, the words more fruity in his mouth.

"All you do is you go down the sewer and you take along some ordinary paper bags, just ordinary brown paper bags, and these bags is filled with plaster of Paris powder. Nothin' else. Then you suspend the bags from the roof of the sewer so they hang down not quite touchin' the water. See? Not quite touchin', and just high enough so a rat can reach 'em."

Claud was listening, rapt.

"There you are, y'see. Old rat comes swimmin' along the sewer and sees the bag. He stops. He takes a sniff at it and it don't smell so bad anyway. So what's he do then?"

"He *gnaws* it," Claud cried, delighted.

"There! That's it! That's exactly it! He starts *gnawin'* away at the bag and the bag breaks and the old rat gets a mouthful of powder for his pains."

"Well?"

"That does him."

"What? Kills him?"

"Yep. Kills him stony!"

"Plaster of Paris ain't poisonous, you know."

"Ah! There you are! That's exackly where you're wrong, see. This powder swells. When you wet it, it swells. Gets into the rat's tubes and swells right up and kills him quicker'n anythin' in the world."

"*No!*"

"That's where you got to know rats."

The ratman's face glowed with a stealthy pride, and he rubbed his stringy fingers together, holding the hands up close to the face. Claud watched him, fascinated.

"Now – where's them rats?" The word "rats" came out of his mouth soft and throaty, with a rich fruity relish as though he were gargling with melted butter. "Let's take a look at them *rraats*."

"Over there in the hayrick across the road."

"Not in the house?" he asked, obviously disappointed.

"No. Only around the hayrick. Nowhere else."

"I'll wager they're in the house too. Like as not gettin' in all your food in the night and spreadin' disease and sickness. You got any disease here?" he asked, looking first at me, then at Claud.

"Everyone's fine here."

"Quite sure?"

"Oh yes."

"You never know, you see. You could be sickenin' for it weeks and weeks and not feel it. Then all of a sudden – bang! – and it's got you. That's why Dr Arbuthnot's so particular. That's why he sent me out so quick, see. To stop the spreadin' of disease."

He had now taken upon himself the mantle of the Health Officer. A most important rat he was now, deeply disappointed that we were not suffering from bubonic plague.

"I feel fine," Claud said, nervously.

The ratman searched his face again, but said nothing.

"And how are you goin' to catch 'em in the hayrick?"

The ratman grinned, a crafty toothy grin. He reached down into his knapsack and withdrew a large tin which he held up level with his face. He peered around one side of it at Claud.

"Poison!" he whispered. But he pronounced it *pye-zn*, making it into a soft, dark, dangerous word, "Deadly *pye-zn*, that's what this is!" He was weighing the tin up and down in his hands as he spoke. "Enough here to kill a million men!"

"Terrifying," Claud said.

"Exackly it! They'd put you inside for six months if they caught you with even a spoonful of this," he said, wetting his lips with his tongue. He had a habit of craning his head forward on his neck as he spoke.

"Want to see?" he asked, taking a penny from his pocket, prising open the lid. "There now! There it is!" He spoke fondly, almost lovingly of the stuff, and he held it forward for Claud to look.

"Corn? Or barley is it?"

"It's oats. Soaked in deadly *pye-zn*. You take just one of them grains in your mouth and you'd be a gonner in five minutes."

"Honest?"

"Yep. Never out of me sight, this tin."

He caressed it with his hands and gave it a little shake so that the oat grains rustled softly inside.

"But not today. Your rats don't get this today. They wouldn't have it anyway. That they wouldn't. There's where you got to know rats. Rats is suspicious. Terrible suspicious, rats is. So today they gets some nice clean tasty oats as'll do 'em no harm in the world. Fatten 'em, that's all it'll do. And tomorrow they gets the same again. And it'll taste so good there'll be all the rats in the districk comin' along after a couple of days."

"Rather clever."

"You got to be clever on this job. You got to be cleverer'n a rat and that's sayin something."

"You've almost got to be a rat yourself," I said. It slipped out in error, before I had time to stop myself, and I couldn't really help it because I was looking at the man at the time. But the effect upon him was surprising.

"There!" he cried. "Now you got it! Now you really said something! A good ratter's got to be more like a rat than anythin' else in the world! Cleverer even than a rat, and that's not an easy thing to be, let me tell you!"

"Quite sure it's not."

"All right, then, let's go. I haven't got all day, you know. There's Lady Leonora Benson asking for me urgent up there at the Manor."

"She got rats, too?"

"Everybody's got rats," the ratman said, and he ambled off down the driveway, across the road to the hayrick and we watched him go. The way he walked was so like a rat it made you wonder – that slow, almost delicate ambling walk with a lot of give at the knees and no sound at all from the footsteps on the gravel. He hopped nimbly over the gate into the field, then walked quickly round the hayrick scattering handfuls of oats on to the ground.

The next day he returned and repeated the procedure.

The day after that he came again and this time he put down the poisoned oats. But he didn't scatter these; he placed them carefully in little piles at each corner of the rick.

"You got a dog?" he asked when he came back across the road on the third day after putting down the poison.

"Yes."

"Now if you want to see your dog die an 'orrible twistin' death, all you got to do is let him in that gate some time."

"We'll take care," Claud told him. "Don't you worry about that."

The next day he returned once more, this time to collect the dead.

"You got an old sack?" he asked. "Most likely we goin' to need a sack to put 'em in."

He was puffed up and important now, the black eyes gleaming with pride. He was about to display the sensational results of his craft to the audience.

Claud fetched a sack and the three of us walked across the road, the ratman leading. Claud and I leaned over the gate, watching. The ratman prowled around the hayrick, bending over to inspect his little piles of poison.

"Somethin' wrong here," he muttered. His voice was soft and angry.

He ambled over to another pile and got down on his knees to examine it closely.

"Somethin' bloody wrong here."

"What's the matter?"

He didn't answer, but it was clear that the rats hadn't touched his bait.

"These are very clever rats here," I said.

"Exactly what I told him, Gordon. These aren't just no ordinary kind of rats you're dealing with here."

The ratman walked over to the gate. He was very annoyed and showed it on his face and around the nose and by the way the two yellow teeth were pressing down into the skin of his lower lip. "Don't give me that crap," he said, looking at me. "There's nothin' wrong with these rats except somebody's feedin' 'em. They got somethin' juicy to eat somewhere and plenty of it. There's no rats in the world'll turn down oats unless their bellies is full to burstin'."

"They're clever," Claud said.

The man turned away, disgusted. He knelt down again and began to scoop up the poisoned oats with a small shovel, tipping them carefully back into the tin. When he had done, all three of us walked back across the road.

The ratman stood near the petrol-pumps, a rather sorry, humble ratman now whose face was beginning to take on a brooding aspect. He had withdrawn into himself and was brooding silence over his failure, the eyes veiled and wicked, the little tongue darting out to one side of the two yellow teeth, keeping the lips moist. It appeared to be essential that the lips should be kept moist. He looked up at me, a quick surreptitious[1] glance, then over at Claud. His nose-end twitched, sniffing the air. He raised himself up and down a few times on his toes, swaying gently, and in a voice soft and secretive, he said: "Want to see somethin'?" He was obviously trying to retrieve his reputation.

"What?"

"Want to see somethin' *amazin'*?" As he said this he put his right hand into the deep poacher's pocket of his jacket and brought out a large live rat clasped tight between his fingers.

"Good God!"

"Ah! That's it, y'see!" He was crouching slightly now and craning his neck forward and leering at us and holding this enormous brown rat in his hands, one finger and thumb making a tight circle around the creature's neck, clamping its head rigid so it couldn't turn and bite.

"D'you usually carry rats around in your pockets?"

"Always got a rat or two about me somewhere."

With that he put his free hand into the other pocket and produced a small white ferret.

"Ferret," he said, holding it up by the neck.

The ferret seemed to know him and stayed still in his grasp.

"There's nothin'll kill a rat quicker'n a ferret. And there's nothin' a rat's more frightened of either."

He brought his hands close together in front of him so that the ferret's nose was within six inches of the rat's face. The pink beady eyes of the ferret stared at the rat. The rat struggled, trying to edge away from the killer.

"Now," he said. "Watch!"

His khaki shirt was open at the neck and he lifted the rat and slipped it down inside his shirt, next to his skin. As soon as his hand was free, he unbuttoned his jacket at the front so that the audience could see the bulge the body of the rat made under his shirt. His belt prevented it from going down lower than his waist.

Then he slipped the ferret in after the rat.

Immediately there was a great commotion inside the shirt. It appeared that the rat was running around the man's body, being chased by the ferret. Six or seven times they went around, the small bulge chasing the larger one, gaining on it slightly

[1] stealthy

each circuit and drawing closer and closer until at last the two bulges seemed to come together and there was a scuffle and a series of shrill shrieks.

Throughout this performance the ratman had stood absolutely still with legs apart, arms hanging loosely, the dark eyes resting on Claud's face. Now he reached one hand down into his shirt and pulled out the ferret; with the other he took out the dead rat. There were traces of blood around the white muzzle of the ferret.

"Not sure I liked that very much."

"You never seen anything' like it before, I'll bet you that."

"Can't really say I have."

"Like as not you'll get yourself a nasty little nip in the guts one of these days," Claud told him. But he was clearly impressed, and the ratman was becoming cocky again.

"Want to see somethin' far more *amazn'n* that?" he asked. "You want to see somethin' you'd never even *believe* unless you seen it with your own eyes?"

"Well?"

We were standing in the driveway out in front of the pumps and it was one of those pleasant warm November mornings. Two cars pulled in for petrol, one right after the other, and Claud went over and gave them what they wanted.

"You want to see?" the ratman asked.

I glanced at Claud, slightly apprehensive. "Yes," Claud said. "Come on then, let's see."

The ratman slipped the dead rat back into one pocket, the ferret into the other. Then he reached down into his knapsack and produced – if you please – a second live rat.

"Good Christ!" Claud said.

"Always got one or two rats about me somewhere," the man announced calmly. "You got to know rats on this job, and if you want to know 'em you got to have 'em round you. This is a sewer rat, this is. An old sewer rat, clever as buggery. See him watchin' me all the time, wonderin' what I'm goin' to do? See him?"

"Very unpleasant."

"What are you going to do?" I asked. I had a feeling I was going to like this one even less than the last.

"Fetch me a piece of string."

Claud fetched him a piece of string.

With his left hand, the man looped the string around one

121

of the rat's hind legs. The rat struggled, trying to turn its head to see what was going on, but he held it tight around the neck with finger and thumb.

"Now!" he said, looking about him. "You got a table inside?"

"We don't want the rat inside the house," I said.

"Well – I need a table. Or somethin' flat like a table."

"What about the bonnet of that car?" Claud said.

We walked over to the car and the man put the old sewer rat on the bonnet. He attached the string to the windshield wiper so that the rat was now tethered.

At first it crouched, unmoving and suspicious, a big-bodied grey rat with bright black eyes and a scaly tail that lay in a long curl upon the car's bonnet. It was looking away from the ratman, but watching him sideways to see what he was going to do. The man stepped back a few paces and immediately the rat relaxed. It sat up on its haunches and began to lick the grey fur on its chest. Then it scratched its muzzle with both front paws. It seemed quite unconcerned about the three men standing near by.

"Now – how about a little bet?" the ratman asked.

"We don't bet," I said.

"Just for fun. It's more fun if you bet."

"What d'you want to bet on?"

"I'll bet you I can kill that rat without usin' my hands. I'll put my hands in my pockets and not use 'em."

"You'll kick it with your feet," Claud said.

It was apparent that the ratman was out to earn some money. I looked at the rat that was going to be killed and began to feel slightly sick, not so much because it was going to be killed but because it was going to be killed in a special way, with a considerable degree of relish.

"No," the ratman said. "No feet."

"Nor arms?" Claud asked.

"Nor arms. Nor legs, nor hands neither."

"You'll sit on it."

"No. No squashin'."

"Let's see you do it."

"You bet me first. Bet me a quid."

"Don't be so bloody daft," Claud said. "Why should we give you a quid?"

"What'll you bet?"

"Nothin'."

"All right. Then it's no go."

He made as if to untie the string from the windshield wiper.

"I'll bet you a shilling," Claud told him. The sick gastric sensation in my stomach was increasing, but there was an awful magnetism about this business and I found myself quite unable to walk away or even move.

"You too?"

"No," I said.

"What's the matter with you?" the ratman asked.

"I just don't want to bet you, that's all."

"So you want me to do this for a lousy shillin'?"

"I don't want you to do it."

"Where's the money?" he said to Claud.

Claud put a shilling piece on the bonnet, near the radiator. The ratman produced two sixpences and laid them beside Claud's money. As he stretched out his hand to do this, the rat cringed, drawing its head back and flattening itself against the bonnet.

"Bet's on," the ratman said.

Claud and I stepped back a few paces. The ratman stepped forward. He put his hands in his pockets and inclined his body from the waist so that his face was on a level with the rat, about three feet away.

His eyes caught the eyes of the rat and held them. The rat was crouching, very tense, sensing extreme danger, but not yet frightened. The way it crouched, it seemed to me it was preparing to spring forward at the man's face; but there must have been some power in the ratman's eyes that prevented it from doing this, and subdued it, and then gradually frightened it so that it began to back away, dragging its body backwards with slow crouching steps until the string tautened on its hind leg. It tried to struggle back further against the string, jerking its leg to free it. The man leaned forward towards the rat, following it with his face, watching it all the time with his eyes, and suddenly the rat panicked and leaped sideways in the air. The string pulled it up with a jerk that must almost have dislocated its leg.

It crouched again, in the middle of the bonnet, as far away as the string would allow, and it was properly frightened now, whiskers quivering, the long grey body tense with fear.

At this point, the ratman again began to move his face closer. Very slowly he did it, so slowly there wasn't really any movement to be seen at all except that the face just happened to be a fraction closer each time you looked. He never took his eyes from the rat. The tension was considerable and I wanted suddenly to cry out and tell him to stop. I wanted him to stop because it was making me feel sick inside, but I couldn't bring myself to say the word. Something extremely unpleasant was about to happen – I was sure of that. Something sinister and cruel and ratlike, and perhaps it really would make me sick. But I had to see it now.

The ratman's face was about eighteen inches from the rat. Twelve inches. Then ten, or perhaps it was eight, and then there was not more than the length of a man's hand separating their faces. The rat was pressing its body flat against the car bonnet, tense and terrified. The ratman was also tense, but with a dangerous active tensity that was like a tight-wound spring. The shadow of a smile flickered around the skin of his mouth.

Then suddenly he struck.

He struck as a snake strikes, darting his head forward with one swift knifelike stroke that originated in the muscles of the lower body, and I had a momentary glimpse of his mouth opening very wide and two yellow teeth and the whole face contorted by the effort of mouth-opening.

More than that I did not care to see. I closed my eyes, and when I opened them again the rat was dead and the ratman was slipping the money into his pocket and spitting to clear his mouth.

"That's what they makes lickerish out of," he said. "Rat's blood is what the big factories and the chocolate-people use to make lickerish."

Again the relish, the wet-lipped, lip-smacking relish as he spoke the words, the throaty richness of his voice and the thick syrupy way he pronounced the word *lickerish*.

"No." he said, "there's nothin' wrong with a drop of rat's blood."

"Don't talk so absolutely disgusting," Claud told him.

"Ah! But that's it, you see. You eaten it many a time. Penny sticks and lickerish bootlaces is all made from rat's blood."

"We don't want to hear about it, thank you."

"Boiled up, it is, in great cauldrons, bubblin' and steamin' and men stirrin' it with long poles. That's one of the big secrets of the chocolate-makin' factories, and no one knows about it – no one except the ratters supplyin' the stuff."

Suddenly he noticed that his audience was no longer with him, that our faces were hostile and sick-looking and crimson with anger and disgust. He stopped abruptly, and without another word he turned and sloped off down the driveway out on to the road, moving with the slow, that almost delicate ambling walk that was like a rat prowling, making no noise with his footsteps even on the gravel of the driveway.

The Hitchhiker

The Hitchhiker

I had a new car. It was an exciting toy, a big BMW 3.3 Li, which means 3.3 litre, long wheelbase, fuel injection. It had a top speed of 129 m.p.h. and terrific acceleration. The body was pale blue. The seats inside were darker blue and they were made of leather, genuine soft leather of the finest quality. The windows were electrically operated and so was the sun-roof. The radio aerial popped up when I switched on the radio, and disappeared when I switched it off. The powerful engine growled and grunted impatiently at slow speeds, but at sixty miles an hour the growling stopped and the motor began to purr with pleasure.

I was driving up to London by myself. It was a lovely June day. They were haymaking in the fields and there were butter-cups along both sides of the road. I was whispering along at seventy miles an hour, leaning back comfortably in my seat, with no more than a couple of fingers resting lightly on the wheel to keep her steady. Ahead of me I saw a man thumbing a lift. I touched the footbrake and brought the car to a stop beside him. I always stopped for hitch-hikers. I knew just how it used to feel to be standing on the side of a country road watching the cars go by. I hated the drivers for pretending they didn't see me, especially the ones in big cars with three empty seats. The large expensive cars seldom stopped. It was always the smaller ones that offered you a lift, or the old rusty ones, or the ones that were already crammed full of children and the driver would say, "I think we can squeeze in one more."

The hitch-hiker poked his head through the open window and said, "Going to London, guv'nor?"

"Yes," I said. "Jump in."

He got in and I drove on.

He was a small ratty-faced man with grey teeth. His eyes were dark and quick and clever, like a rat's eyes, and his ears were slightly pointed at the top. He had a cloth cap on his head and he was wearing a greyish-coloured jacket with enormous pockets. The grey jacket, together with the quick eyes and the pointed ears, made him look more than anything like some sort of a huge human rat.

"What part of London are you headed for?" I asked him.

"I'm goin' right through London and out the other side," he said. "I'm goin' to Epsom, for the races. It's Derby Day today."

"So it is," I said. "I wish I were going with you. I love betting on horses."

"I never bet on horses," he said. "I don't even watch 'em run. That's a stupid silly business."

"Then why do you go?" I asked.

He didn't seem to like that question. His little ratty face went absolutely blank and he sat there staring straight ahead at the road, saying nothing.

"I expect you help to work the betting machines or something like that," I said.

"That's even sillier," he answered. "There's no fun working them lousy machines and selling tickets to mugs. Any fool could do that."

There was a long silence. I decided not to question him any more. I remembered how irritated I used to get in my hitch-hiking days when drivers kept asking *me* questions. Where are you going? Why are you going there? What's your job? Are you married? Do you have a girl-friend? What's her name? How old are you? And so on and so forth. I used to hate it.

"I'm sorry," I said. "It's none of my business what you do. The trouble is, I'm a writer, and most writers are terrible nosey parkers."

"You write books?" he asked.

"Yes."

"Writin' books is okay," he said. "It's what I call a skilled trade. I'm in a skilled trade too. The folks I despise is them that spend all their lives doin' crummy old routine jobs with no skill in 'em at all. You see what I mean?"

"Yes."

"The secret of life," he said, "is to become very very good at somethin' that's very very 'ard to do."

"Like you," I said.

"Exactly. You and me both."

"What makes you think that *I'm* any good at my job?" I asked. "There's an awful lot of bad writers around."

"You wouldn't be drivin' about in a car like this if you weren't no good at it," he answered. "It must've cost a tidy packet, this little job."

"It wasn't cheap."

"What can she do flat out?" he asked.

"One hundred and twenty-nine miles an hour," I told him.

"I'll bet she won't do it."

"I'll bet she will."

"All car makers is liars," he said. "You can buy any car you like and it'll never do what the makers say it will in the ads."

"This one will."

"Open 'er up then and prove it," he said. "Go on, guv'nor, open 'er right up and let's see what she'll do."

There is a roundabout at Chalfont St Peter and immediately beyond it there's a long straight section of dual carriage-way. We came out of the roundabout on to the carriage-way and I pressed my foot hard down on the accelerator. The big car leaped forward as though she'd been stung. In ten seconds or so, we were doing ninety.

"Lovely!" he cried. "Beautiful! Keep goin'!"

I had the accelerator jammed right down against the floor and I held it there.

"One hundred!" he shouted ... "A hundred and five!... A hundred and ten!... A hundred and fifteen! Go on! Don't slack off!"

I was in the outside lane and we flashed past several cars as though they were standing still – a green Mini, a big cream-coloured Citroën, a white Land-Rover, a huge truck with a container on the back, an orange-coloured Volkswagen Minibus ...

"A hundred and twenty!" my passenger shouted, jumping up and down. "Go on! Go on! Get 'er up to one-two-nine!"

At that moment, I heard the scream of a police siren. It was so loud it seemed to be right inside the car, and then a policeman on a motor-cycle loomed up alongside us on the inside lane and went past us and raised a hand for us to stop.

"Oh, my sainted aunt!" I said. "That's torn it!"

The policeman must have been doing about a hundred and thirty when he passed us, and he took plenty of time slowing down. Finally, he pulled into the side of the road and I pulled in behind him. "I didn't know police motor-cycles could go as fast as that," I said rather lamely.

"That one can," my passenger said. "It's the same make as yours. It's a BMW R90S. Fastest bike on the road. That's what they're usin' nowadays."

The policeman got off his motor-cycle and leaned the machine sideways on to its prop stand. Then he took off his gloves and placed them carefully on the seat. He was in no hurry now. He had us where he wanted us and he knew it.

"This is real trouble," I said. "I don't like it one bit."

"Don't talk to 'im any more than is necessary, you understand," my companion said. "Just sit tight and keep mum."

Like an executioner approaching his victim, the policeman came strolling slowly toward us. He was a big meaty man with a belly, and his blue breeches were skin-tight around his enormous thighs. His goggles were pulled up on to the helmet, showing a smouldering red face with wide cheeks.

We sat there like guilty schoolboys, waiting for him to arrive.

"Watch out for this man," my passenger whispered. "'Ee looks mean as the devil."

The policeman came round to my open window and placed one meaty hand on the sill. "What's the hurry?" he said.

"No hurry, officer," I answered.

"Perhaps there's a woman in the back having a baby and you're rushing her to hospital? Is that it?"

"No, officer."

"Or perhaps your house is on fire and you're dashing home to rescue the family from upstairs?" His voice was dangerously soft and mocking.

"My house isn't on fire, officer."

"In that case," he said, "you've got yourself into a nasty mess, haven't you? Do you know what the speed limit is in this country?"

"Seventy," I said.

"And do you mind telling me exactly what speed you were doing just now?"

I shrugged and didn't say anything.

When he spoke next, he raised his voice so loud that I jumped. "*One hundred and twenty miles per hour!*" he barked. "That's *fifty* miles an hour over the limit!"

He turned his head and spat out a big gob of spit. It landed on the wing of my car and started sliding down over my beautiful blue paint. Then he turned back again and stared hard at my passenger. "And who are you?" he asked sharply.

131

"He's a hitch-hiker," I said. "I'm giving him a lift."

"I didn't ask you," he said. "I asked him."

"'Ave I done somethin' wrong?" my passenger asked. His voice was as soft and oily as haircream.

"That's more than likely," the policeman answered. "Anyway, you're a witness. I'll deal with you in a minute. Driving-licence," he snapped, holding out his hand.

I gave him my driving-licence.

He unbuttoned the left-hand breast-pocket of his tunic and brought out the dreaded book of tickets. Carefully, he copied the name and address from my licence. Then he gave it back to me. He strolled round to the front of the car and read the number from the number-plate and wrote that down as well. He filled in the date, the time and the details of my offence. Then he tore out the top copy of the ticket. But before handing it to me, he checked that all the information had come through clearly on his own carbon copy. Finally, he replaced the book in his tunic pocket and fastened the button.

"Now you," he said to my passenger, and he walked around to the other side of the car. From the other breast-pocket he produced a small black notebook. "Name?" he snapped.

"Michael Fish," my passenger said.

"Address?"

"Fourteen, Windsor Lane, Luton."

"Show me something to prove this is your real name and address," the policeman said.

My passenger fished in his pockets and came out with a driving-licence of his own. The policeman checked the name and address and handed it back to him. "What's your job?" he asked sharply.

"I'm an 'od carrier."

"A *what*?"

"An 'od carrier."

"Spell it."

"H-O-D-C-A- . . ."

"That'll do. And what's a hod carrier, may I ask?"

"An 'od carrier, officer, is a person 'oo carries the cement up the ladder to the bricklayer. And the 'od is what 'ee carries it in. It's got a long 'andle, and on the top you've got two bits of wood set at an angle . . ."

"All right, all right. Who's your employer?"

"Don't 'ave one. I'm unemployed."

The policeman wrote all this down in the black notebook. Then he returned the book to its pocket and did up the button.

"When I get back to the station I'm going to do a little checking up on you," he said to my passenger.

"Me? What've I done wrong?" the rat-faced man asked.

"I don't like your face, that's all," the policeman said. "And we just might have a picture of it somewhere in our files." He strolled round the car and returned to my window.

"I suppose you know you're in serious trouble," he said to me.

"Yes, officer."

"You won't be driving this fancy car of yours again for a very long time, not after *we've* finished with you. You won't be driving *any* car again come to that for several years. And a good thing, too. I hope they lock you up for a spell into the bargain."

"You mean prison?" I asked, alarmed.

"Absolutely," he said, smacking his lips. "In the clink. Behind the bars. Along with all the other criminals who break the law. *And* a hefty fine into the bargain. Nobody will be more pleased about that than me. I'll see you in court, both of you. You'll be getting a summons to appear."

He turned away and walked over to his motor-cycle. He flipped the prop stand back into position with his foot and swung his leg over the saddle. Then he kicked the starter and roared off up the road out of sight.

"Phew!" I gasped. "That's done it."

"We was caught," my passenger said. "We was caught good and proper."

"I was caught, you mean."

"That's right," he said. "What you goin' to do now, guv'nor?"

"I'm going straight up to London to talk to my solicitor," I said. I started the car and drove on.

"You mustn't believe what 'ee said to you about goin' to prison," my passenger said. "They don't put nobody in the clink just for speedin'."

"Are you sure of that?" I asked.

"I'm positive," he answered. "They can take your licence away and they can give you a whoppin' big fine, but that'll be the end of it."

I felt tremendously relieved.

"By the way," I said, "why did you lie to him?"

"Who, me?" he said. "What makes you think I lied?"

"You told him you were an unemployed hod carrier. But you told *me* you were in a highly skilled trade."

"So I am," he said. "But it don't pay to tell everythin' to a copper."

"So what *do* you do?" I asked him.

"Ah," he said slyly. "That'd be tellin', wouldn't it?"

"Is it something you're ashamed of?"

"Ashamed?" he cried. "Me, ashamed of my job? I'm about as proud of it as anybody could be in the entire world!"

"Then why won't you tell me?"

"You writers really is nosey parkers, aren't you?" he said. "And you ain't goin' to be 'appy, I don't think, until you've found out exactly what the answer is?"

"I don't really care one way or the other," I told him, lying.

He gave me a crafty little ratty look out of the sides of his eyes. "I think you do care," he said. "I can see it on your face that you think I'm in some kind of a very peculiar trade and you're just achin' to know what it is."

I didn't like the way he read my thoughts. I kept quiet and stared at the road ahead.

"You'd be right, too," he went on. "I *am* in a very peculiar trade. I'm in the queerest peculiar trade of 'em all."

I waited for him to go on.

"That's why I 'as to be extra careful 'oo I'm talking' to, you see. 'Ow am I to know, for instance, you're not another copper in plain clothes?"

"Do I look like a copper?"

"No," he said. "You don't. And you ain't. Any fool could tell that."

He took from his pocket a tin of tobacco and a packet of cigarette papers and started to roll a cigarette. I was watching him out of the corner of one eye, and the speed with which he performed this rather difficult operation was incredible. The cigarette was rolled and ready in about five seconds. He ran his tongue along the edge of the paper, stuck it down and popped the cigarette between his lips. Then, as if from nowhere, a lighter appeared in his hand. The lighter flamed. The cigarette was lit. The lighter disappeared. It was altogether a remarkable performance.

"I've never seen anyone roll a cigarette as fast as that," I said.

"Ah," he said, taking a deep suck of smoke. "So you noticed."

"Of course I noticed. It was quite fantastic."

He sat back and smiled. It pleased him very much that I had noticed how quickly he could roll a cigarette. "You want to know what makes me able to do it?" he asked.

"Go on then."

"It's because I've got fantastic fingers. These fingers of mine," he said, holding up both hands high in front of him, "are quicker and cleverer than the fingers of the best piano player in the world!"

"Are you a piano player?"

"Don't be daft," he said. "Do I look like a piano player?"

I glanced at his fingers. They were so beautifully shaped, so slim and long and elegant, they didn't seem to belong to the rest of him at all. They looked more like the fingers of a brain surgeon or a watchmaker.

"My job", he went on, "is a hundred times more difficult than playin' the piano. Any twerp can learn to do that. There's titchy little kids learnin' to play the piano in almost any 'ouse you go into these days. That's right, ain't it?"

"More or less," I said.

"Of course it's right. But there's not one person in ten million can learn to do what I do. Not one in ten million! 'Ow about that?"

"Amazing," I said.

"You're darn right it's amazin'," he said.

"I think I know what you do," I said. "You do conjuring tricks. You're a conjurer."

"Me?" he snorted. "A conjurer? Can you picture me goin' round crummy kids' parties makin' rabbits come out of top 'ats?"

"Then you're a card player. You get people into card games and you deal yourself marvellous hands."

"Me! A rotten card-sharper!" he cried. "That's a miserable racket if ever there was one."

"All right. I give up."

I was taking the car along slowly now, at no more than forty miles an hour, to make quite sure I wasn't stopped again. We had come on to the main London-Oxford road and were running down the hill toward Denham.

Suddenly, my passenger was holding up a black leather belt in his hand. "Ever seen this before?" he asked. The belt had a brass buckle of unusual design.

"Hey!" I said. "That's mine, isn't it? It *is* mine! Where did you get it?"

He grinned and waved the belt gently from side to side. "Where d'you think I got it?" he said. "Off the top of your trousers, of course."

I reached down and felt for my belt. It was gone.

"You mean you took it off me while we've been driving along?" I asked, flabbergasted.

He nodded, watching me all the time with those little black ratty eyes.

"That's impossible," I said. "You'd have had to undo the buckle and slide the whole thing out through the loops all the way round. I'd have seen you doing it. And even if I hadn't seen you, I'd have felt it."

"Ah, but you didn't, did you?" he said, triumphant. He dropped the belt on his lap, and now all at once there was a brown shoelace dangling from his fingers. "And what about this, then?" he exclaimed, waving the shoelace.

"What about it?" I said.

"Anyone around 'ere missin' a shoelace?" he asked, grinning.

I glanced down at my shoes. The lace of one of them was missing. "Good grief!" I said. "How did you do that? I never saw you bending down."

"You never saw nothin'," he said proudly. "You never even saw me move an inch. And you know why?"

"Yes," I said. "Because you've got fantastic fingers."

"Exactly right!" he cried. "You catch on pretty quick, don't you?" He sat back and sucked away at his home-made cigarette, blowing the smoke out in a thin stream against the windshield. He knew he had impressed me greatly with those two tricks, and this made him very happy. "I don't want to be late," he said. "What time is it?"

"There's a clock in front of you," I told him.

"I don't trust car clocks," he said. "What does your watch say?"

I hitched up my sleeve to look at the watch on my wrist. It wasn't there. I looked at the man. He looked back at me, grinning.

"You've taken that, too," I said.

He held out his hand and there was my watch lying in his palm. "Nice bit of stuff, this," he said. "Superior quality. Eighteen-carat gold. Easy to flog, too. It's never any trouble gettin' rid of quality goods."

"I'd like it back, if you don't mind," I said rather huffily.

He placed the watch carefully on the leather tray in front of him. "I wouldn't nick anything from you, guv'nor," he said. "You're my pal. You're givin' me a lift."

"I'm glad to hear it," I said.

"All I'm doin' is answerin' your question," he went on. "You asked me what I did for a livin' and I'm showin' you."

"What else have you got of mine?"

He smiled again, and now he started to take from the pocket of his jacket one thing after another that belonged to me – my driving-licence, a key-ring with four keys on it, some pound notes, a few coins, a letter from my publishers, my diary, a stubby old pencil, a cigarette-lighter, and last of all, a beautiful old sapphire ring with pearls around it belonging to my wife. I was taking the ring up to the jeweller in London because one of the pearls was missing.

"Now *there's* another lovely piece of goods," he said, turning the ring over in his fingers. "That's eighteenth century, if I'm not mistaken, from the reign of King George the Third."

"You're right," I said, impressed. "You're absolutely right."

He put the ring on the leather tray with the other items.

"So you're a pickpocket," I said.

"I don't like that word," he answered. "It's a coarse and vulgar word. Pickpockets is coarse and vulgar people who only do easy little amateur jobs. They lift money from blind old ladies."

"What do you call yourself, then?"

"Me? I'm a fingersmith. I'm a professional fingersmith." He spoke the words solemnly and proudly, as though he were telling me he was the President of the Royal College of Surgeons or the Archbishop of Canterbury.

"I've never heard that word before," I said. "Did you invent it?"

"Of course I didn't invent it," he replied. "It's the name given to them who's risen to the very top of the profession. You've 'eard of a goldsmith and a silversmith, for instance. They're experts with gold and silver. I'm an expert with my fingers, so I'm a fingersmith."

"It must be an interesting job."

"It's a marvellous job," he answered. "It's lovely."

"And that's why you go to the races?"

"Race meetings is easy meat," he said. "You just stand around after the race, watchin' for the lucky ones to queue up and draw their money. And when you see someone collectin' a big bundle of notes, you simply follows after 'im and 'elps yourself. But don't get me wrong, guv'nor. I never takes nothin' from a loser. Nor from poor people neither. I only go after them as can afford it, the winners and the rich."

"That's very thoughtful of you," I said. "How often do you get caught?"

"Caught?" he cried, disgusted. "*Me* get caught! It's only pickpockets get caught. Fingersmiths never. Listen, I could take the false teeth out of your mouth if I wanted to and you wouldn't even catch me!"

"I don't have false teeth," I said.

"I know you don't," he answered. "Otherwise I'd 'ave 'ad 'em out long ago!"

I believed him. Those long slim fingers of his seemed able to do anything.

We drove on for a while without talking.

"That policeman's going to check up on you pretty thoroughly," I said. "Doesn't that worry you a bit?"

"Nobody's checkin' up on me," he said.

"Of course they are. He's got your name and address written down most carefully in his black book."

The man gave me another of his sly, ratty little smiles. "Ah," he said. "So 'ee 'as. But I'll bet 'ee ain't got it all written down in 'is memory as well. I've never known a copper yet with a decent memory. Some of 'em can't even remember their own names."

"What's memory got to do with it?" I asked. "It's written down in his book, isn't it?"

"Yes, guv'nor, it is. But the trouble is, 'ee's lost the book. 'Ee's lost both books, the one with my name in it *and* the one with yours."

In the long delicate fingers of his right hand, the man was holding up in triumph the two books he had taken from the policeman's pockets. "Easiest job I ever done," he announced proudly.

I nearly swerved the car into a milk-truck, I was so excited.

"That copper's got nothing on either of us now," he said.

"You're a genius!" I cried.

"'Ee's got no names, no addresses, no car number, no nothin'," he said.

"You're brilliant!"

"I think you'd better pull in off this main road as soon as possible," he said. "Then we'd better build a little bonfire and burn these books."

"You're a fantastic fellow," I exclaimed.

"Thank you, guv'nor," he said. "It's always nice to be appreciated."

Points for Discussion and Suggestions for Writing

(Suggestions for writing are marked with an asterisk.)

Man from the South

1 Where do you imagine the story is set and how does the author use description of setting to add to the atmosphere?

2 What clues are there in the early part of the story that the Man from the South is a little out of the ordinary?

3 What aspects of the man's behaviour lead the narrator to observe, "I had the feeling he was relishing a private little secret all his own?"

4 How does the Man from the South set about encouraging the American cadet to bet with his cigarette lighter? How do the cadet's reactions to the challenge change as they discuss the bet?

5 Why does the writer introduce the girl friend into the story and what does her presence contribute to the action?

6 What is there in the old man's actions that suggest "the son of a bitch had done this before"? How does the author emphasise the ritual involved and the rising tension?

7 Why, at the end of the story, does the wife smile "a slow sad smile"?

*8 We are told that in the past he has taken forty-seven fingers from different people and has lost eleven cars. Why might the Man from the South have developed such a strange obsession? Write the story of the very first time he won "a pound of flesh".

*9 Imagine you are next in line with this bizarre man, and write the story of how you were persuaded into betting, what the bet was, and how it concluded.

*10 Holidays often take us into foreign countries where we encounter people and customs we are not used to. What unusual experiences have you shared while away from home? You might write this in the form of a newspaper article, a diary, short story or narrative poem.

*11 Suggestions for further writing:
Strange Meeting

Encounters of a Third Kind
Torture!
The Bet
It Never Fails
A Pound of Flesh
Obsessions
'Oh, not again!'
The Severed Head

Lamb to the Slaughter

1 What sort of story does the title lead us to expect? When is the phrase "lamb to the slaughter" usually used?

2 What sort of household do we imagine the Maloney home to be? How does Roald Dahl evoke a homely atmosphere and why is the sense of domestic peace recalled at the end of the tale?

3 Before the husband breaks the news, what clues are there that this particular evening is going to be a break with routine? What do you think Mr Maloney actually says to his wife?

4 Are Mrs Maloney's reactions and actions after the murder believable? How are we first informed that she is planning to establish an alibi, and what is that alibi to be?

5 Is it reasonable that the policemen should be fooled by what she says (remember she is a policeman's wife) or do you find the whole thing rather unlikely? Is the story less enjoyable for being implausible?

6 Why does the writer concentrate on such detail as "their voices thick and sloppy because their mouths were full of meat"?

7 Both "Man from the South" and this story end with dramatic irony. Explain what is meant by "dramatic irony" – what other examples can you think of from other stories or plays you have read?

8 Mrs Maloney commits what her lawyer might call "a crime of passion". Does that justify her crime and what would your verdict be if you were a jury member at her trial?

9 The fact that she is pregant perhaps makes us feel more sympathetic towards Mary Maloney. She asks herself, "What were the laws about murderers with unborn children? Did they kill them both – mother and child?" This is an interesting question and you might like to research the topic,

reporting back for a class debate on capital punishment.

*10 Construct a detective thriller story in which there is a most unusual murder weapon, or a plot which has an ironic final twist.

*11 Write a short play – no more than three scenes – in which someone in your family arrives home with some shattering news. Try to describe the actions and reactions of every member of the family.

*12 Suggestions for further writing:
Routine
The Homecoming
"I hope you won't blame me too much . . . "
The Trance
Shock
The Alibi
Get the Weapon and You've Got the Man
Do Me a Favour
Breaking Up
The Unborn
Police!

The Landlady

1 What impression do we get of Billy Weaver from the opening paragraphs? How are his character and personality an important part of the story?

2 The author gives us details of some ordinary, some extra-ordinary features of the landlady's house. What are these and what do they contribute to the narrative?

3 As the story develops we learn more about Billy Weaver. Pick out phrases which help us build up a portrait of him.

4 In "Man from the South" the narrator guesses that the old man had been through the finger-chopping ritual before. How might we guess that the landlady has also rehearsed her actions for a previous client? Why does the author use italics for certain words when the landlady speaks?

5 Which phrases would lead us to conclude that the landlady is "slightly off her rocker"? Why does the writer wish to make her seem dotty, almost simple and innocent?

6 What leads Billy to observe that the landlady "had probably lost a son in the war and had never got over it"?

7 What hints to "get out fast" might Billy have picked up if he were less naive? Do you think in his position you would

have been equally gullible?

8 What is the peculiar smell that lingers in the house and in the tea?

9 The landlady turns out to be a macabre taxidermist. Find out all you can about this profession – there are certain to be some strange stories linked with it.

10 Roald Dahl uses a lot of similes in the story in order to create a chilling atmosphere; for example, "the wind was *like* a flat blade of ice on his cheeks", and "each word was *like* a large black eye". Pick out other similes which you feel add to the effectiveness of the story and look carefully at how the writer describes people and places in great detail. It might be useful to compare the words and phrases used in this story with those found in "Galloping Foxley" or "The Ratcatcher", both of which contain very vivid descriptions of events and characters.

*11 Billy thinks he may have read about Mulholland and Temple in the newspapers. Write the article describing their strange disappearance. Write a follow-up piece about Billy Weaver, perhaps linking the three young men with a story and theory that emphasise mystery and intrigue for your readers.

*12 At the end of the story the landlady will have three "preserved" young men. Imagine you are the landlady – what might she write in her diary each day? Tell the tale of the next unhappy victim – perhaps this time she meets with some resistance!

*13 Suggestions for further writing:
A New Job
Bed and Breakfast
First Day Away From Home
The Visitors' Book
The Attic-Room
Poison!
Bodies. Bodies!
Anyone For Tea?
The Taxidermist
Dead or Alive

The Champion of the World

1 Before the word "poaching" is mentioned how might we guess that Claud and Gordon are about to do something illegal and perhaps dangerous?

2 How are we informed that Claud is a master poacher and how does the writer create a sense of history surrounding the art of poaching?

3 How does the author make the whole story seem a private war between Victor Hazel and the rest of the village? Whose side is the narrator on and how can you tell?

4 Claud describes the different ways of catching pheasants with obvious enjoyment and sincerity. Gordon at first doesn't believe what he says. Do you think the poaching methods seem realistic or are they pure fantasy?

5 Write a fuller description of Victor Hazel's hunting party – you may want to exaggerate a little – based on the description that they were "debilitated gentlemen in tweed suits". What sort of attitude does the author want us to have towards them?

6 "Poachers on sighting game ... are like women who sight large emeralds in a jeweller's window, the only difference being that the women are less dignified in the methods they employ later on to acquire the loot." What does the author seem to be saying here about both women and poachers?

7 How does the writer make the whole night adventure comic, yet at the same time conveying the excitement and danger of poaching? Make a list of phrases which help build up the tension.

8 What sort of picture are we given of the gamekeepers, and why are they presented in this particular way?

9 At the end of the story, as Bessie Organ is "closing fast", how does the writer highlight the comedy? Which phrases and descriptions are particularly effective?

10 Who is the Champion of the World in this story? Or is it just an ironic title?

*11 Bessie Organ tries to transport only half of their enormous catch of pheasants. Write a follow-up scene describing what happens to the remaining birds stored in her coal shed. Remember that she is the local vicar's wife!

12 In one of Roald Dahl's stories for children, "The Magic Finger", there is a girl who turns huntsmen into ducks so that they can feel what it is like to be shot at. In another book, *Fantastic Mr Fox*, animals completely outwit humans. Do you think the writer is siding with the pheasants in this story? Discuss the arguments for and against hunting and culling. Is poaching a special case?

144

*13 Dahl wrote a longer version of this same story for children and called it "Danny the Champion of the World". It is very funny and well worth reading. Imagine you were expanding the plot. Write a few extra scenes and try to make them both humorous and realistic.

*14 Imagine you have spent a long time carefully plotting a crime. Write the story (funny or serious) of the crime when something goes disastrously wrong.

*15 Suggestions for further writing:
The Strangest Invention
Disguise
Night Walk
The Crusade
Genius
A Dream Come True
Loot
A Tall Story
The Gamekeeper
The Crooked Vicar

Galloping Foxley

1 How does the narrator emphasise that he is a creature of habit? Why does he like the "unchanged and unchangeable" fellow travellers?

2 What seem to be the main characteristics of the people he passes during his daily walk from Cannon Street to the office? In what way are their lives "regulated nicely by the minute hand of an accurate watch"?

3 The narrator says that his kind of people are the businesslike folk. What does he mean by "these so-called clever types who want to tip the world upside-down"? Do you imagine people who work in the City feel the same way as the narrator?

4 Roald Dahl constructs this story so that he starts off with a very ordinary scene and then introduces something dramatic. Many of his stories work in this way. Do you find it effective and entertaining or rather unlikely?

5 In what ways are we told that the stranger "was not one of us"?

6 Why do different newspapers feature in the story? Do we associate certain things with particular newspapers, and if so what?

7 What seem to you to have been the worst things that Perkins

had to suffer at school? Why didn't he write home to his parents telling them the truth?

8 Does Perkins want to expose the stranger in front of other commuters because he envies the stranger's good looks or because he wants a sort of revenge? Or is it just "a little impish fancy"?

9 Do you think the stranger really is who he says he is or, is it in fact Galloping Foxley trying to avoid being discovered? What might you have done in a similar situation?

10 Perkins says at the beginning of the story that the whole episode proved to be "rather peculiar". How would you describe the story and do you think that Perkins learnt any lessons at the end?

11 Would "The Contented Commuter" have made a better title? What other titles might fit the storyline?

*12 Using the very detailed descriptions we are given of both Perkins and the stranger, write a character sketch of each, perhaps bringing out their worst features.

13 Do you agree with Perkins that "there's nothing like routine and regularity for preserving one's peace of mind"? What are the advantages and disadvantages of organising your life around a routine?

14 If you think that Perkins paints an exaggerated picture of life at a Public School, you might like to read Roald Dahl's descriptions of his boarding school education at Repton where the Headmaster, later to become the Archbishop of Canterbury, regularly beat pupils with great gusto. Dahl writes in "Lucky Break" (an autobiographical essay): "To my certain knowledge this future Head of the Church of England once had to produce a basin of water, a sponge and a towel so that the victim could wash the blood away afterwards." Why do you think the schools allowed this sort of behaviour from teachers and pupils? What are your views about corporal punishment?

*15 Imagine that the stranger becomes a regular commuter on Perkins's train. Write two or three follow-up scenes from Perkins's point of view.

*16 Suggestions for further writing:
Train Journeys
City Life
The Contented Commuter
Stranger

First Day at School
The Dormitory
Pain!
Mistaken Identity
Loneliness
True Friends
Dying a Thousand Deaths

Mrs Bixby and the Colonel's Coat

1 What does the writer mean by saying that "America is the land of opportunities for women"? Does his picture of contemporary America seem realistic, and might it even be true of British society today?

2 This is story within a story; the author writes to a particular formula and we know in advance that the husband is going to turn the tables on his wife. Does the action seem less exciting and entertaining because we know this in advance, or is the final scene all the more satisfying because of the way the plot is constructed?

3 Mrs Bixby says that she feels "a sort of eternal patient, someone who dwelt in the waiting-room". What does this tell us about their married life?

4 After Mrs Bixby reads the Colonel's note she experiences a variety of feelings which the author captures in single words and sentences. Do you find this style of writing effective here? Make a list of her changing emotions.

5 What sort of person do you imagine the pawnbroker to be and how do he and Mrs Bixby react to each other?

6 Why does Mrs Bixby describe her husband as a "bluff"? How are we told that Mr Bixby is very involved with his work? Try writing a character sketch of both husband and wife, emphasising their differences.

7 Are there any signs in Mr Bixby's words about the pawn ticket, and later when he presents the fur, that he has guessed what is going on and is deliberately tricking his wife?

8 How does Mrs Bixby fit the formula (given at the beginning) of the woman who is "flabbergasted, stupefied, humiliated, defeated"?

9 Is this yet another story where Dahl leaves the reader satisfied with how things have worked out? Does it depend on whether you are male or female when it comes to taking sides with either Mr or Mrs Bixby?

10 This tale is well worth studying in detail for the way it is constructed and how a writer handles ideas, actions and characters. For example, the framework of telling a story within a story, letting the reader know in advance what the likely outcome will be, getting characters to reveal their inner thoughts; work though the text and try to analyse any interesting aspects of style you come across. As a longer project, compare this story with others in the volume which employ different storytelling techniques.

*11 In *The Importance of Being Earnest*, a play by Oscar Wilde, one of the characters, whenever he wants to escape from friends, pretends that he is going to visit a sick relative in the country. He calls this "Bunburying", and it is exactly what Mrs Bixby does to trick her husband. How do you escape from people you don't want to see or from jobs you have to do? Write a story with this theme of Bunburying.

*12 Imagine you have been expecting an expensive present, something you have long waited for; when it arrives you are bitterly disappointed for some reason. Try to describe your feelings in a short essay.

*13 Suggestions for further writing:
New York, New York!
The Dirty Dog
The Problems of Divorce
Working Like A Slave
The Mad Dentist
The Letter
A Pawn Ticket . . .
Surprise, Surprise!
A Lady/Gentleman Friend

Skin

1 What does the story gain from being told partly as a flash-back?

2 When the writer is describing the life that Drioli, his wife and Soutine shared, how does he convey both their poverty and their great happiness? What does this add to the rest of the narrative and to the reader's feelings at the end?

3 What does Soutine mean when he says about his paintings, "They are not nourishing. I cannot eat them"? Describe Soutine as you imagine him to be.

4 When Drioli lays out the tattooing instruments and starts

demonstrating with them, what does the writer want us to feel?

5 Why is Drioli stunned by the tattoo that Soutine creates? Why is it ironic that the picture turns out so well?

6 What do you think gives Drioli "a sudden impulse" to enter the gallery? How does the writer convey the wealth of the gallery patrons and also their disdain towards the intruder?

7 What is there about the owner of the Hotel Bristol which finally wins Drioli? Why does Dahl end the story with the narrator talking about a maid bringing Drioli "breakfast in bed in the mornings"? What similarities are there with the concluding lines of "The Landlady"?

8 "How quickly the sight of one small object such as this can stir the memory." In "Skin" and "Galloping Foxley" a glimpse at something or someone triggers off memories. Are these memories too detailed to be realistic or are they a convenient way of developing a story? Can you think of any occasions where you have experienced a similar jogging of the memory? Do you recall happy or sad events more easily?

9 One of the men in the gallery says, "Perhaps, if one were to offer this old man enough money, he might consent to kill himself on the spot." Do you think Drioli is so blinded by the offer of comfort and food that he doesn't guess exactly what he is doing by going to the Hotel Bristol? Will people do almost anything for money? Discuss some of the jobs you would never do, at any price.

*10 How do you think Drioli met his end? Write the gruesome story of his final days, his death and how the picture "nicely framed and heavily varnished" came to be stretched!

11 Do you find the story amazing, unbelievable, funny, sickening or a mixture of these? Drioli, with his tattoo, is clearly a human freak; society tends to treat physical disability either as a joke or as something disturbing and untouchable. What are your views on the subject?

12 Roald Dahl gives us the impression that the art world is both wealthy and unscrupulous. In recent years, a painter called Tom Keating has tried to expose the corrupt practices of art dealers and in doing so was brought to trial. Find out more about him and prepare a discussion on the subject of forged paintings and the sale of works of art. You could also research into the art of the tattoist.

*13 Suggestions for further writing:

The Ratcatcher

1 Why does the ratcatcher call himself the "rodent operative"?

2 How and why does the author make him seem like the animals he hunts? What indications are there in the story that the ratman is inseparable from his trade?

3 "A most important rat he was now, deeply disappointed that we were not suffering from bubonic plague." What does this tell us about the personality of the ratcatcher and his attitude towards non-experts?

4 Does the ratman seem a believable character or a caricature? Do you think the writer exaggerates with details such as the ratman's pronunciation of "pye-zn"?

5 Why does the ratcatcher want to show Claud his tricks? Do you feel he succeeds in his aim?

6 How does the author make the reader share the ratcatcher's gambling enthusiasm, and what means does he employ to establish the terrible tension between man and rat?

7 The ratcatcher leaves the filling station exactly as he arrives – "like a rat prowling, making no noise with his footsteps even on the gravel of the driveway". What does the story gain by having this kind of circular plot?

8 Why do you imagine the ratcatcher describes in detail what rat's blood can be made into? Compare your "gut reaction" to this story with your response to "Skin". Are you, like those watching the ratcatcher, disgusted? Or are you fascinated, even faintly amused?

*9 Why do you suppose the skilled ratcatcher failed to catch any rats? This story is one of four grouped under the general title of "Claud's Dog", and if you want to discover the inevitably ghoulish reason why the rats don't feed on the poisoned oats, you should read the complete tale. Try writing the scene that takes place the following day when the ratman arrives and discovers the truth. Let your imagination wander . . .

10 It is difficult to picture a more horrific sight than a man biting off an animal's head. Describe the most sickening thing you have ever seen.

11 Suggestions for further writing:
Nightmare
Party Tricks
Blood-Sports
The Amazing Adventures Of . . .
The Outsider
The Unbelievable Happened
Hidden In The Hay
Plague

The Hitchhiker

1 What impression of the narrator does the writer wish us to form at the start of the story and why?

2 Compare the descriptions of the ratcatcher in the previous story and the hitchhiker? Do you think the author is saying something about judging people by their appearance? Remembering the lesson of "Galloping Foxley", do you think you can judge people's characters and personalities from their appearance? Think about your parents, friends and teachers.

3 How do the occupants of the car differ in their reactions to the policeman and why?

4 How does it help the story that the writer dwells on the unpleasant attitude of the patrolman?

5 The ratcatcher describes himself as a "rodent operative", the pick-pocket calls himself a "fingersmith"; in the same way a dustman is often known as a "refuse collector". Why are more complicated terms used when a simple word is adequate?

6 Why, if the fingersmith is a criminal, do we end up admiring him? How are we told that he is proud of his profession and how does he justify his crimes?

7 Unlike the other stories in this volume, "The Hitchhiker" ends on a very happy note for one of the characters. Why are such endings rare in Roald Dahl's writing, and do you feel this story is less successful as a result?

*8 Would you agree with the fingersmith when he says that "the secret of life is to become very very good at somethin' that's very 'ard to do"? If you had the chance, what would you choose to excel at and why? Write the newspaper report which describes yourself as Champion of the World.

*9 Suggestions for further writing:

My Dream Car/Motor-Bike
The Lonely Road
The Guv'nor
A Day At The Races
Tales Of A Hitchhiker
Speed Kills
Fantastic Fingers
A Gambling Man
The Little Black Book
Freedom

General questions

*1 Which is your favourite story? Write a review recommending it to other readers, remembering to examine the plot, characters, setting, style of writing and what makes it funny, frightening or satisfying.

*2 Roald Dahl seems to be pre-occupied with elements of the fantastic – ratcatchers, fingersmiths, tattooists. Of the many unusual characters in these stories which lingers longest in your mind? Write a short character sketch of that person, using the story's details as a starting point and adding your own impressions to round off the description.

*3 The writer establishes many moments of great terror and horror. Use any one scene which you recall vividly as a starting point for a short story of your own.

4 When you look back over a story it is always difficult to decide at which point in the narrative you realised what the ending might be. Try doing this with these stories, exploring the text for clues (or red herrings) left by the writer.

5 Judging by this selection what seem to you to be the author's favourite subjects? Do you like the titles he has given or could you think of more suitable ones?

*6 Several of the stories were filmed for a television series called *Tales of the Unexpected*. What do you think generally might be lost or gained in transferring the tales to the screen? Try writing your own television/film script for one of the shorter stories, including details of setting, sound effects, music, character casting and camera angles.

7 Most of the stories start off with descriptions of very ordinary

surroundings and everyday routines; then suddenly terror or surprise is introduced. What do the stories gain or lose by following this formula?

*8 Does the author make you sympathise with what happens to his characters and do the conclusions leave you satisfied? Try rewriting one of the stories putting yourself in the place of one of the characters – you may decide to react differently from the way Roald Dahl describes the action.

*9 *Longer Project.* If you are presenting a folder of work or an in-depth study about the writer you may like to follow some of these suggestions:

Analyse critically Dahl's narrative techniques and style of writing.

Rewrite some of the stories, or scenes from them, in the form of a diary, newspaper article, play, filmscript, long poem.

Group the titles of his stories into themes.

Research into biographical details of the writer.

Take photographs or draw scenes to accompany the stories.

Collect news and reviews from magazines, newspapers and book jackets about the writer and his publications.

Design a suitably "fantastic" folder.

Reading and Writing Short Stories

It is important to remember that the short story is not just an unfinished novel, a book in which the author ran out of ideas – it is a form or "genre" of fiction in its own right. While a novelist tries to explore a number of themes the short-story writer is working out a single idea and often rounding off with a simple yet satisfying dénouement. The most popular form of story is one that tells a tale, recounting a series of events with a definite beginning, middle and end. Other writers, for example James Joyce in his finely evocative *Dubliners*, offer a "slice of life": a snapshot of human beings caught up in their everyday routine or at a moment of crisis.

But the real art in telling a short story lies in creating the right kind of balance; the writer has to beware of telling the reader too much and thereby weakening the final effect. H. E. Bates, author of over six hundred short stories, summed this up by saying: "The short story must depict more by implication than by statement, more by what is left out than left in. . . . Writing a short story may be compared with building a house with matchsticks. There comes a point in its construction when the addition of another stick may well bring down the whole affair in ruins." Characters are therefore often sketched in such a way that while the reader is not told everything, yet by the end of the story he has learned enough by implication to picture them clearly.

So how does the writer set about constructing his story? He must concern himself with character, setting, plot and he has at his disposal all sorts of devices to control the way the story unfolds on the page. To start with he has to make a selection because the short story does not have the space to tell a complete life-story. Will it be the peculiar, the lonely, the eccentric, the downright mad or the plain ordinary which focuses his attention? Depending on the type of story the writer will then decide to tell it in one of two ways; either the events can be arranged in a straight chronological sequence building up to a climax, or he can begin part way through the story and use flashbacks.

In "The Landlady", "The Ratcatcher" and "Man from the South" Roald Dahl wants to lead his reader through a series of actions to a dramatic climax; in "Galloping Foxley" and "Skin" the sight of someone or something triggers off memories which are told as a flashback, while Mrs Bixby's story is different again because the author tells us in advance the probable outcome.

The author can also choose from a number of different narrative devices. He can decide to write in the first person, the "I" form, as though one person is witnessing events, a device which adds great immediacy. "The Champion of the World", "Man from the South" and "The Hitchhiker" employ this style, with the added dimension in "The Hitchhiker" that the "I" might well be Roald Dahl himself, caught for speeding and luckily encountering the fantastic fingersmith. Another device is to tell the story as though it is all seen through a third person, but as with the first-person narrative, this means that the reader can only be told what one particular character knows and thinks – we cannot see into the minds of other characters. "Lamb to the Slaughter" for example is told through Mary Maloney, and we are made to share her agonies and enjoy her final satisfaction at having tricked her dead husband's colleagues.

But if the author wants to be able to inform his reader what everyone in the story is thinking and doing then he must act as the all-seeing narrator, and to his narrative he will inevitably add a point of view, a certain tone in the telling. Thus in "Mrs Bixby and the Colonel's Coat" Dahl wants us to sympathise with the man whose wife is unfaithful and constructs the story in such a way that we know from the outset what will happen, and when it does we are well satisfied. In real life we come to judge someone's personality from a whole range of actions and words, and our conclusions about fictional characters are formed in a similar way. We note what the character says about himself, how he thinks and acts, what other characters say about him and what the narrator might say – only then is the portrait complete.

In developing the storyline the author must ensure that the reader's attention is engaged from the outset. Some short-story writers consistently invent dramatic openings, whereas Roald Dahl tends to start the narrative with an often unexciting, deliberative paragraph in which the "ordinariness" of life is emphasised, and suddenly introduces the unexpected or the unusual a page later. "In the afternoon the ratcatcher came to the filling station", for example, in no way prepares us for the scene in which the rodent operative decapitates the rat with his own mouth, and the beginnings of "Lamb to the Slaughter" and "Man from the South" are similarly deceptive. The writer must also, either through dialogue or description, drop hints and give clues so that the ending does not appear too implausible. Dahl often does this with dramatic short sentences – "A leg of lamb", "It said BED AND BREAKFAST", "The cane! That did it!" – which at once fire the reader's imagination and serve in the progression of the plot.

Looking back through a short story it is instructive to pick out those lines which on first reading might appear quite harmless but which turn out to be pointing inevitably towards the climax; in "The Landlady" Billy Weaver is "compelled" to enter the boarding house, in "The Hitchhiker" the first appearances of the fingersmith afford clues to his identity, while in "Lamb to the Slaughter" there is the dramatically ironic clue in the detective's words "Get the weapon, and you've got the man." Equally important for the short-story writer are his concluding lines, and in Dahl's writing the brilliantly timed, constantly astonishing finales are one of the most memorable features of his style.

A short story must have people in action and their actions are often the working out of the author's ideas and interests. Each author will have his own favourite topics, largely dependent on that vital mixture of personal experiences and imaginative fantasy, and the reader will often come to "know" a writer through a familiarity with these favourite themes. H. E. Bates, the prolific short-story writer, is known for his tales of the countryside he loved, while James Joyce celebrated and criticised his native Dublin on every page he wrote. Roald Dahl lists gambling as one of his real life loves, and so it comes as no surprise that "Man from the South" and "The Ratcatcher" revolve around the making of wagers. Another Dahl story "The Wonderful Story of Henry Sugar" describes the life of a man who learns to see through playing cards; in another, "Dip in the Pool", a character bets his life's savings on the speed of the boat in which he is travelling, and in "Taste" a wine expert gambles for a daughter's hand in marriage. In each case, the endings are predictably unpredictable.

In this selection the writer's fascination with nightmarish pain and death is evident with the leg of lamb murder, the stuffing of Billy Weaver, the tattoo in "Skin". Elsewhere in Dahl's fictional world, a husband rots to death in a lift, a jealous husband saws off his wife's neck, and in a story titled simply "Pig" a vegetarian on a guided tour of a meat-processing factory suddenly and bloodily ends up as sausage meat! Getting revenge, as in "Galloping Foxley"; the battle of the sexes in the tale of the Bixbys; the "extraordinary" in the doping of pheasants and the magic fingers; the pathos of human frailty, the tiny action which disturbs many lives – all these are recurrent themes which the reader can identify and thereby better "know" his author.

Your own writing

In his autobiographical essay "Lucky Break" Roald Dahl lists some of the qualities which he thinks a fiction writer should have: the ability to write well, to make a scene come alive in the reader's mind; stamina to stick at writing hour after hour, month after month; strong self-discipline because there is no one going to sack you if you don't turn up for work; a keen sense of humour; a degree of humility; a lively imagination; and he must be a perfectionist, never being satisfied with what he has written until it has been re-written again and again.

Even if you are not going to be a professional writer, it is worth remembering these qualities in your own everyday compositions. It is also important to bear in mind many of the techniques which have been explained in this chapter. Your choice of subject will be based on personal experiences and on your imagination. The story can be funny, odd, horrible, sad, happy, romantic, tender or disgusting, but it needs a carefully developed plot, an awareness of the different narrative devices, the establishing of character, lively dialogue and detailed descriptions. You should try to state your point of view and sympathies either implicitly or explicitly, and aim to thrill, puzzle, excite and exhilarate the reader. Finally, here is a checklist of questions to ask yourself before you put pen to paper:

What do you want to say in the story?

Where is it happening?

How important are the details of location?

Who is telling the story?

How many characters are involved?
What do the characters know about each other?
How much do you want the reader to know and how much do
    you want to surprise him or her?

Further Reading

For those who would like to read more stories of the macabre and fantastic, the following editions in Penguin paperback are easily available:

Someone Like You. Contains fifteen stories, five of which are included in this Imprint.

Kiss Kiss. Contains eleven stories – three are included in this volume.

Over To You. Subtitled "Ten stories of flyers and flying". These are among the first Roald Dahl wrote and are based on his experiences as a wartime fighter pilot.

Switch Bitch. Four long short stories, with strong sexual elements.

The Wonderful Story of Henry Sugar and six more. Includes "The Hitchhiker" and the autobiographical essay "Lucky Break".

For children he has written:
James and the Giant Peach
Charles and the Chocolate Factory
Charlie and the Great Glass Elevator
Fantastic Mr Fox
The Magic Finger
Danny the Champion of the World

My Uncle Oswald, Michael Joseph. This is the author's first novel.

Other Writers

The following are just a brief selection from the great wealth of short-story writers who may be of interest to readers who have enjoyed Roald Dahl:

BARSTOW, STAN, *The Human Element and other stories*, Longman Imprint Books.

BATES, H. E., *The Good Corn and other stories*, Longman Imprint Books.

BRADBURY, RAY, *To Sing Strange Songs*, Wheaton, Literature for Life.

GRAVES, ROBERT, *The Shout and Other Stories*, Penguin.

GREENE, GRAHAM, *Twenty-one Stories*, Penguin.

HILL, SUSAN, *A Bit Of Singing And Dancing*, Penguin.

JOYCE, JAMES, *A James Joyce Selection*, Longman Imprint Books.

LAWRENCE, D. H., *Selected Short Stories*, Penguin.

MAUPASSANT, GUY. *Selected Short Stories*, Penguin Classics.

MUNRO, H. H., *Saki*, Picador.

O'CONNOR, FRANK, *My Oedipus Complex*, Penguin.

SCOTT, FITZGERALD, F., *The Diamond As Big As The Ritz and Other Stories*, Penguin.

SILLITOE, ALAN, *A Sillitoe Selection*, Longman Imprint Books.

THURBER, JAMES, *Vintage Thurber*, Hamish Hamilton.

There are also many other collections of short stories in the series in which this book is published. A full list of Longman Imprint Books follows, on pages 161 and 162.

Longman Imprint Books

General Editor: Michael Marland CBE MA
Titles in the series
There is a Happy Land Keith Waterhouse
The Human Element Stan Barstow
* **The Leaping Lad and other stories** Sid Chaplin
Conflicting Generations Five television scripts
* **A Sillitoe Selection** *edited by* Michael Marland
* **Late Night on Watling Street and other stories** Bill Naughton
Black Boy Richard Wright
Scene Scripts Seven television plays
The Experience of Work *edited by* Michael Marland
The Kraken Wakes John Wyndham
A Hemingway Selection *edited by* Dennis Pepper
Ten Western Stories *edited by* C.E.J. Smith
The Experience of Sport *edited by* John L. Foster
Loves, Hopes and Fears, *edited by* Michael Marland
Cider with Rosie Laurie Lee
The Pressures of Life Four television plays
Goalkeepers are Crazy Brian Glanville
A James Joyce Selection *edited by* Richard Adams
Out of the Air Five radio plays *edited by* Alfred Bradley
Scene Scripts Two Five television plays
Caribbean Stories *edited by* Michael Marland
An Isherwood Selection *edited by* Geoffrey Halson
A Thomas Hardy Selection *edited by* Geoffrey Halson
While they Fought *edited by* Michael Marland *and* Robin Willcox
The Wave and other stories Liam O'Flaherty
Irish Short Stories *edited by* Frances Crowe
The Experience of Parenthood *edited by* Chris Buckton
The Experience of Love *edited by* Michael Marland
Twelve War Stories *edited by* John L. Foster
A Roald Dahl Selection *edited by* Roy Blatchford
A D H Lawrence Selection *edited by* Geoffrey Halson
I'm the King of the Castle Susan Hill
Sliding Leslie Norris
Still Waters Three television plays by Julia Jones
Scene Scripts Three Four television plays *edited by* Roy Blatchford
Television Comedy Scripts Five scripts *edited by* Roy Blatchford
Juliet Bravo Five television scripts
Meetings and Partings Sixteen short stories *compiled by* Michael Marland
Women compiled *and edited by* Maura Healy
Strange Meeting Susan Hill
Looks and Smiles Barry Hines
A Laurie Lee Selection *edited by* Chris Buckton
P'tang, Yang, Kipperbang and other TV plays Jack Rosenthal
Family Circles Five plays *edited by* Alfred Bradley *and* Alison Leake
Humour and Horror Twelve plays *edited by* Caroline Bennitt
Scene Scripts Four Four television plays *edited by* Alison Leake
A Second Roald Dahl Selection *edited by* Helene Fawcett
Scene Scripts Five Four television plays *edited by* Alison Leake
Race to be Seen *edited by* Alison Leake and Mark Wheeller
Festival Plays *edited by* Margaret Mackey
Dash and Defiance *edited by* Alison Leake

* Cassette available